To David

SALAMONIE FARM

NOAH HERSHBERGER

Noah Hershberg

Goosefoot Acres Press
CLEVELAND, OHIO

ISBN: 1-879863-53-7

Illustrations by Chris S. Koehler

Lyrics to *How Great Thou Art* on p. 149 (© Copyright by S. K. Hine 1953, renewed 1981) used by permission of Manna Music, Inc, 35255 Brooten Road, Pacific City, OR 97135. All rights reserved.

Copies Available From Noah Hershberger
7080 Marvin Rd., Holton, MI 49425
(231) 821-9131

Library of Congress Cataloging-in-Publication Data

Hershberger, Noah.
   Salamonie Farm / Noah Hershberger ; [illustrations by Chris S. Koehler].
      p.   cm.
   Summary: A fictionalized account of a year in the life of an Amish farm family, as seen through the eyes of the six-year-old son.
    ISBN 1-879863-53-7 (alk. paper)
    [1. Amish--Fiction. 2. Farm life--Fiction. 3. Family life--Fiction.] I. Koehler, Chris S., ill.   II. Title.
PZ7.H432423Sa 1 1996
[Fic]--dc20   96-2695
                                                                                   CIP
                                                                                    AC

Goosefoot Acres Press
Division of Goosefoot Acres, Inc.
P.O. Box 18016
Cleveland, OH 44118-0016
(216) 932-2145

To
Dad, Mom and my brothers and sisters
whom I shall never forget

Preface

Homesickness probably brought *Salamonie Farm* to life. After moving hundreds of miles away from my family, writing about my brothers, sisters and parents was an excellent therapy for that illness.

It took the help of various people to bring this book to its present level. First, I am grateful to my teachers who taught me to use reference books and make outlines, and, most of all, assigned many compositions. Sincere thanks also go to Clif Bushnel, a long-time friend, who served as the link that connected me to Goosefoot Acres Press. Thanks also go to Peter Gail and his staff at Goosefoot Acres Press for their persistent and patient labor in evaluating, editing and producing this work.

This story combines the experience of my brother, myself, and what I am observing as I involve my own children in the work of our farm. As all of us didn't share exactly the same upbringing, the book has purposely been written as "fiction" to more completely portray the range of experiences young children have growing up on an Amish farm. For those of you who grew up on farms, I hope reading this book will bring back some fond memories of your earlier life. It certainly has for me.

Noah Hershberger
Hillpoint, Wisconsin
December 1995

Contents

Prologue

It may be confusing to say that a big cornfield was on a little farm. But, to a 6-year-old boy walking behind a horse-drawn cultivator, 23 acres definitely looks big. On the other hand, when we compare an 80 acre family farm with todays corporate agri-business complex, with its hundred-plus cow dairy farm or its thousand-plus acre cash cropper or its enormous hog operation, we come out with a "little farm."

Another paradox of the "little farms" was that the family could be poor and still live a reasonably comfortable life. There wasn't much money with which to buy things, but there was lots of meat and vegetables, and plenty of practical knowledge about how to prepare them. So when growing boys came in from a day of exercise on the farm, all hollow and "hungry as wolves", delicious, filling meals were waiting for them.

The story you are about to read is based on my reminiscences of life on one of those small farms. Our family is Amish, and, consequently, most of the work was done by hand or with simple machinery drawn by horses. At that time, although tractors and motorized machinery were coming into use fast, many other farmers still did their work that way as well.

As a child and even now, I have always been fascinated by tales of long ago. My parents' accounts of their childhood and the stories handed down to them never cease to hold my attention. Although this story happened less than fifty years ago, in this age of fast change things are very different even in many Amish homes than they were then.

In 1953, when the story begins, the American Middle West was simply decked with little farms. Eighty to one hundred sixty acres was considered a normal-sized family farm. Almost every operation had cows, pigs, chickens, sheep, and maybe even horses. Things have changed dramatically since then. Now most of the animals are gone. Many of the little farms have disappeared. Fences have been torn out, buildings have been razed, and the cash crop farmer has taken over the land.

East of Pennville, Indiana, by a curve on old Highway 22, was a little farm. It, too, is gone. In 1994, when I visited the site, the whole farm was one big cornfield. The concrete of the milk and pump houses and the two culverts of the half circle driveway were all that was left. A passerby would never dream that a beautiful home once stood there, but memories tell us that once upon a time it was a family farm.

Chapter 1

Farm Home

Home was on the little farm in Eastern Indiana. The year was 1953. Sammie, who was going on 6, was the oldest of the four children, and his world wasn't very big. He had heard Dad talk about Ohio, and Mom had told the children about Tennessee where her parents lived, but those places were far away. Sammie's world was mostly on the little farm.

As far as anyone could see to the north or to the east or to the west were other farms. There were barnyards of cattle and sheep and pigs. Almost every farm had a chicken house full of laying hens. Fields of beautiful oats, barley, wheat, hay and corn waved in the summer winds. Here and there, often on the edges of or encircling the fields, were plots of woodland, most of which were made up of dense stands of oak and hickory and walnut trees. Cedar and maple trees grew in these woods, too, as well as elm and ash. That, and the pastures, completed the picture. It was beautiful farm country.

The land all around was "flat as a pancake," as Dad said. To the south were more farms, but beyond those the land gently dropped down to the lowlands along the Salamonie River. Sammie could see the low tree line of the groves that stood along the bank of the river, but that was the limit of his experience. He had no idea that the river continued on toward the northwest, growing larger and larger as it meandered toward the place where it joined the Wabash River .

Mom had grown up on these Indiana prairies, and the children — Sammie, Lydia, Dannie, and Baby David — were growing up here, too. Only Dad had grown up far away in the rolling hills of Holmes County, Ohio.

In those days and on that little farm, the children knew about hard work. Dad was very busy caring for all the cows and pigs and chickens and horses, plus he had to plant the crops and harvest them. Sammie was old enough to be his helper. Also, Mom needed a lot of fuel for the kitchen stove, since she kept a fire going in it all day to cook their three meals as well as to bake bread, pies and cookies in between. So Sammie helped her too. He and Lydia carried in armful after armful of firewood and pail after pail of dry corncobs.

On the little farm there was, in addition to the hard work, hard luck and hard times. Hard luck was when animals got sick or storms or drought hurt the crops, or when wild animals sneaked up from the woods and killed chickens, and the hard luck seemed to bring on the hard times. Sammie sometimes thought about the wild animals as he lay in his bed at night. He knew that an animal had to be very quiet or Sport, their black retriever dog, would hear it. After thinking about it for awhile, Sammie could almost see an animal sneaking through the dark. Quickly he pulled his quilt over his head, and shivered. Just then Sport would bark, and Sammie knew that whatever was out there was being chased back to the woods where it belonged.

Sometimes Dad had to go out at night when he heard the chickens squawking. Sammie was glad to stay in the house at those times. He just snuggled underneath the blankets of his warm bed upstairs and listened. Once a raccoon got into the henhouse and killed some chickens.

Dad went out quickly with his shotgun, but the raccoon got away. The next day Dad had to fix the hole where the raccoon had entered, so the next time Mr. Coon sneaked up from the woods, he had to go back home without a chicken. Sammie was glad about that.

All summer long the children went barefoot, but when winter was coming, shoes were a must. Every year Dad and Mom had to save and stretch to get enough money to buy shoes for everyone, and somehow they did. One fall day each year, Dad and Mom got out the Sears & Roebuck catalog. They measured four sets of little feet and ordered shoes, but it always seemed to take a long time for the shoes to arrive. Every day the children would watch for the mailman until he finally brought them a large box.

New shoes, as a once-a-year deal, were a special treat. They were nice and shiny, but the children had to be careful not to look at them too much. If they caught each other looking, they would remind (or maybe even accuse) one another of "being proud". A goodly amount of arguing and discussion always followed the arrival of new shoes.

Not all was hard work. Dad and Mom believed that "all work and no play makes dull boys and girls." After the work was done, there was lots of time to play. Sometimes Dad brought home a little candy, and Mom's home-cooked meals were delicious.

Sometimes on summer evenings after a hard day of work, the family relaxed on the porch which was attached to the front of their large square farm house. In the front yard was a huge old oak tree, with branches that reached out and made nice shade over the front lawn and porch. It was a cool place to be in hot weather. If the children didn't feel like sitting, they could play in the yard and still be in the cool shade of that friendly old tree.

The half-circle driveway ran past the house and on out past the two chicken houses, the milkhouse, the tall red barn, the shed and the granary. It made a wide curve and continued back to the road.

There were corn fields all around. A gravel road ran to the south, and along its edges, ragweed stood as tall as the corn. The ragweed waved back and forth and the short, recently cut grass by the road vibrated as the wind blew through it.

All day long cars and trucks went up and down Highway 22. They slowed down for the curve in front of the little farm, then picked up speed and drove on. Sammie knew that across the road and a little to the east lived Herman Gressingers. They were the closest neighbors.

Further east the highway took them to the Eli Mullets' and on from there to Uncle Andys'. The Mullets were neighbors and good friends of Dad and Mom, and their son Oley was Sammie's age. The highway to the west took them to town. Across the fields to the southwest lived the Orin Grabers. That was Sammie's world.

Dad sometimes traded work with Orin Graber. They called it "neighboring back and forth." Orin was a jolly man, and Sammie liked him, but his boys, Freeman and Abner, played rough and Sammie dreaded when the two families got together.

Once when they were at Orins' for Sunday dinner, Freeman was sitting on the bench against the wall. People were sitting on both sides of him, and the table was in front, but he began getting up to leave the table anyway.

"Just stay seated," Orin told him, "Not everyone is finished eating, yet."

But Freeman waited no longer. He stood up on the bench and walked right over the table. Orin looked at him sternly but said nothing.

Sammie saw Dad and Mom looking at each other across the table. They would never allow Sammie, Lydia or Dannie do such a thing. The children had to mind their manners or they'd get a spanking!

Around the farm the children had to watch out for bees. Dad had two hives behind the chicken house, and bees from these hives came to visit the white clover blossoms that grew on the lawn around the house. When the children walked through the grass with bare feet, they had to be very careful to keep from being stung. Once Sammie got stung on the foot. It hurt, and he cried.

"Don't cry, Sammie," Dad said, "You're not as bad off as the bee."

"What?" Sammie asked.

"The poor bee left its stinger in your foot," Dad said, pointing to the spot on the foot, "When bees do that, they die."

Dad took out his pocket knife and carefully pulled out the little black stinger, being very careful not to squeeze it. Bees have a venom in their stinger, Dad told Sammie, and if the stinger is squeezed before it is pulled out, more of the venom is pushed into the wound. That makes it hurt worse and swell up more.

Sammie went into the house and showed the bee sting to Mom. She knew just what to do; she just took a bottle of white liniment from the medicine cabinet and put some on the wound. That immediately took away the sharp pain, and soon the foot was better.

Another thing the children had to watch out for was strange dogs.

"Always stay away from them," Dad told them, "You never know when one shows up with rabies." He told them what he knew about rabies, "An animal with rabies usually goes wild and bites or attacks anything in its path. Then it keeps getting sicker and sicker until it dies."

"Sport would chase such an animal away," Sammie said.

"Well, that may not be so good. When a person or animal gets bitten by a rabid animal, it spreads to them. They also get rabies, and could die unless they go through a very painful and long treatment," Dad explained, "So we don't want Sport to get bitten."

So stray dogs were watched with suspicion. You could never tell when one would show up with rabies.

Inside the farmhouse there was nothing to fear. All was snug and safe, and Sport was outside keeping watch. He wasn't much of a cow dog, but the whole family loved him. He caught rats and groundhogs and chased marauding animals back to the woods, which was a help to Dad. He barked whenever people came, and Mom liked that. The children loved to stroke his soft silky black fur. Whenever they took a drink to Dad in the fields, they took Sport along. They felt safe with him.

At night Sammie lay in his bed listening to the sounds outside. Through the screen in his upstairs bedroom window, he could hear the leaves of the oak tree whispering back and forth. He could hear the cows mooing and the horses whinnying. When Sport barked, Sammie knew that someone or something had come too close to the little farm. Once he heard a terrible screech that made shivers run up and down his spine. Quickly he jumped out of bed and ran downstairs to Dad and Mom's bedroom.

"Dad, did you hear that screech" he asked fearfully.

"Yes, Sammie," Dad answered sleepily, "It is only a screech owl. It won't hurt you. Go back to bed and go to sleep."

Sammie went back upstairs to bed, but lay awake. He didn't think that he could ever get used to the sound of the screech owl. It was a terrible thing to hear in the dark. He pulled the covers up over his head and shivered. But in the snug warmth of his bed and the safety of the house, he soon fell fast asleep.

..... milk, fresh milk ..... side cans and ..... people always drank a ..... sweet, foamy milk. They also ..... when ..... after it ..... made ..... so warm by the ..... fresh milk and ..... sold it milk ..... for the children.

Chapter 2

Watching the Cows

There were six milk cows on the farm. The two oldest cows were favorites of the children because they were gentle. Bessie was a fawn colored Jersey. She stood at the end of the stable so it was easy to pet her. In the next stall stood a beautiful brindle cow named Rose. The rest of the herd were also good cows, but the children didn't pay as much attention to them because they weren't as tame.

Twice a day Dad and Mom milked the cows by hand. They poured the milk through a strainer into ten gallon cans. After milking, Dad set the cans on a two-wheeled milk cart and pushed them to the milkhouse which stood between the house and the barn. There he lowered them into the cooling tank, and started the gas engine that ran the pump outside. Good cold water from the well flowed through a large gray pipe into the cooling tank. This cooled the warm milk and kept it cool until the milk truck arrived to pick it up.

Every day except Sunday the truck came to pick up the fresh milk. No milk was sold on Sunday because that was the Lord's Day, a day for resting and going to church. No work was done except chores and no business was discussed. In warm weather the Saturday evening milk couldn't be kept fresh until Monday, so it wasn't sold. Instead Dad set the cans just outside the milkhouse door and went inside to put together the mechanical cream separator.

When the children saw him doing that, they came running. Dad would dip out fresh milk from the cans and give them each all they wanted. Sammie always drank a cup or two of that good, sweet, foamy milk. They also drank milk when Mom served it at the table, but after it was cooled, it didn't taste the same as it did warm from the cows. The children loved fresh milk and Mom said it made red cheeks on little children.

Then Dad cranked the handle of the separator and, using a milk pail, he poured the milk into the hopper at the top. Out of one spout flowed the white skim milk, which was fed to the pigs. Out of the other, and into a glass gallon jar, flowed a thin stream of rich, golden cream. When the jar was full, Dad set it in the water trough to cool.

Later Mom would take the cream to the house and pour it into her glass butter churn. Taking turns, the children would sit on the floor and turn the handle of the churn. At first it was fun to watch the cog wheels turn the wooden paddle, which made the cream slosh around in the churn. But it took a long time to make butter and the children soon became bored with the job.

"Do we have to keep cranking?" Sammie would ask then.

"Not at all," Dad would answer, smiling, "All you have to do is become willing, then you don't have to."

That was an old joke that Dad always played on the children. When you weren't willing to do something but had to do it anyway, it was always harder than if you were able to find something about the job which made it fun. So, even though Sammie couldn't find anything good about the job, and was very tired of it, he kept on turning the handle because he had to.

Finally Dad came in for dinner and took over the job. He began turning the handle, and before long, little pieces of butter began forming inside the churn. As the pieces of butter became larger, he began rocking the handle back and forth to work the pieces together. When he stopped, Mom poured the contents of the churn into her large wooden butter bowl and worked out the buttermilk with a wooden paddle. When she was done, she had a hunk of pure, yellow butter to be spread on slices of good home-made bread and a jar of buttermilk, which she set aside to use in her baking recipes. In winter the butter was hard, but now it was soft and creamy.

It was late summer. The oats and barley had been cut and threshed, leaving only the bottom part of the plants, or stubble, standing short and stiff in the field. For over a month there had been no rain and it was very hot and dry. The pasture and hay fields were brown, and the cows had grazed the grass down to the bare earth, leaving nothing more to eat. Grasses and clover and weeds were growing nice and green in the stubble field, so Dad decided to use that for pasture. However, there was no fence along one side, and someone would have to watch so the cows didn't get into the corn.

"Come with me," Dad said. He showed Sammie and Lydia how to walk along the corn field and keep the cows away.

"Here," he said, giving them each a stick, "Wave your sticks and show them you mean business."

Then Dad went back to the barn.

At first it was fun. Every time a cow came near the cornfield, they ran at her waving their sticks. The cow always turned and ran away. The more she ran, the more the children enjoyed it.

"You must not make the cows run," Dad said when he took them out the next day.

Of course they had to obey. But now it wasn't so much fun. Soon Sammie sat down by the edge of the field and let Lydia chase the cows.

"You have to help!" she complained after a while.

"Okay," Sammie agreed, "You take a turn a little while longer yet, then I will watch them.

"Okay," she agreed a little reluctantly, and went back to chasing cows. When all the cows were a good distance away, she came back and flopped down exhausted next to Sammie.

"Now it IS your turn!" she declared, wiping the sweat from her face. The dust from her hands mixed with the sweat and some of it had stayed.

"I wish we had some water back here," Lydia sighed and again tried to wipe her hot forehead.

"Okay," Sammie volunteered, "I'll watch the cows now and you can go to the house for water."

"No, 'cause Dad said we have to watch the cows," Lydia disagreed.

"But Dad didn't think about us getting thirsty. I think he would say it is all right to get water if he knew we were thirsty," Sammie reasoned.

Lydia wasn't sure. Slowly she got to her feet and a bit uncertainly began walking toward the house.

Sammie looked at the cows eating grass. A few of them were getting close to the corn field. He knew he should go chase them, but it was a hot day. He was thirsty and didn't feel like getting up just yet. Maybe Lydia would soon be back with a drink. Then he would feel more like chasing cows.

Suddenly he saw Dad coming from the barn on the run. He looked around and immediately knew why Dad was running. Two cows were eating corn by the edge of the field and all the other cows were walking swiftly that way, too! Now Sammie did jump up in a hurry! What would Dad say? How he wished he had done better, but it was too late. He ran over and helped chase the cows away.

"Why didn't you watch them?" Dad asked sternly.

Sammie looked at the ground. "It-it is so-so warm," he stuttered.

"Well yes, it is warm," Dad answered, "but being out here for an hour shouldn't be that bad. Where is Lydia?"

"She went to get some water to drink," Sammie answered.

"It is only for an hour that you have to watch the cows. I was coming to put them back into the pasture just now. You shouldn't have to go get a drink in that amount of time. It is important that you keep the cows out of the cornfield. Otherwise, they will spoil the corn and we won't have enough for the cows next winter," Dad said, and he began herding the cows toward the gate.

Sammie felt terrible! He had not done what Dad had told him to. Suppose too much corn was spoiled already!

The next day the children got a drink from the pump before they went to watch the cows.

"Make sure you watch them," Dad said before they left.

That day was just as hot as the one before. Sport lay next to the corn in the shade and panted away as only a dog can pant. The children were miserable, but they watched the cows. After an hour Dad came and put the cows back into the pasture.

Every day they watched the cows. Along the side of the stubble field the yellow goldenrod tops were ablaze with color. Hundreds of swallows glided through the air and bunched together to begin their long flight to the sunny south. Dad said those were signs that fall wasn't far away.

Sammie heard a sound which he didn't recognize and asked Dad about it.

"That is the seventeen-year locust," Dad explained as they listened to it's raspy song. He caught one and showed it to the children. Sammie looked at the large shiny bug with its red eyes and red wing veins. It was amazing that it could make such a loud, raspy sound.

Dad told them what he knew about the locust. "This year they will lay eggs in trees. When the little worms hatch, they fall to the ground and live in the soil and eat roots. In another seventeen years they will be grown into adult locusts. That will be another locust year."

Sammie thought about that. Seventeen years seemed like a long, long time. "How old will I be then?" he asked.

Dad thought a little then he said, "You will be twenty-two years old then." Sammie couldn't imagine that. Twenty-two seemed pretty old.

One day while they were watching the cows, a strange dog came suddenly out of the corn field not far away. It was a big dog, bigger than Sport, bigger than any dog Sammie had ever seen, and it stood there looking at the children. It had a large mouth and its red tongue hung out as it panted in the summer heat. Sammie looked at its shaggy, grayish-black coat and his heart seemed to jump into his throat and stick there. But what he saw next made the blood drain from his face! One, two, three, four, five more strange dogs came out of the corn! What if they had rabies? What if they came after the children or bit Sport or the cows?

He grabbed Sport's collar and held fast. But Sport didn't want to be held. A low growl came from deep inside his throat. He pulled with all his might and Sammie had to let go. The children both stood speechless as Sport ran toward the dogs. In a moment there would surely be a terrible fight and Sport didn't have a chance against a whole pack.

But then something very unexpected happened. From behind him, Sammie heard Dad yell and he turned to see him running toward them. The strange dogs all quickly turned and made a beeline for the woods at the back of the field with Sport in hot pursuit.

"I wish I'd had my gun," Dad said when he arrived, gasping for breath.

The dogs disappeared into the woods and were gone.

Sport gave up the chase and came trotting back across the field. He happily flopped down at Dad's feet and the children stroked his soft fur.

When they returned to the house after putting in the cows, the children heard Dad telling Mom about the dogs.

"Other people around the neighborhood have been seeing them, too. They killed three of Howard Strait's sheep over close to town, and another farmer caught them chasing his hogs. No telling what they would have done here if I had not come upon them when I did. That leader is part wolf or I'll miss my guess."

"Is it safe for the children to watch the cows?" Mom asked.

The children listened wide-eyed. Sammie knew he didn't want to go back there again without Dad.

"The grass in the stubble field is about gone anyway," he heard Dad say, "I guess we'll start feeding hay in the barn."

The children were happy about that. For days they stayed close to the house. Even then they kept a wary eye on the woods and the cornfields. No telling when those dogs would come back.

In the following week the family heard more about the dogs. Here and there a neighbor would spot them going into a corn field, and they were seen prowling around hog pens. One farmer had some sheep killed. Always that big gray leader was the king of the pack. Dad said he was "sly as a fox" and they always managed to get away, even though the sheriff kept driving up and down the country roads looking for them.

Chapter 3

Neighborhood Frolic

They kept wishing for rain. The leaves in the woods had started changing color and the large oak tree in front of the house had begun to turn red. Dad said that any rain that would come now wouldn't do much good for this year, because soon there would be frost and not much more grass would grow.

Dad had been talking about raising calves for sale, but to do this, he needed to build a lean-to on the barn to house them. They had calves on the farm already, but Dad was planning to buy more and raise them to sell. He needed money to buy hats and shoes and groceries and cloth so Mom could make pants and shirts for Dad and Sammie and Dannie, as well as clothes for Baby David and dresses for herself and Lydia. Those things all took money and Dad didn't have much. Raising calves, he said, seemed to be a good way to make extra money.

Dad began hauling lumber in from town with the team and wagon. When he came home with the first load, he told the family, "A farmer south of town caught that dog pack in his hog house. He closed it up and called the sheriff."

"So they are all caught?" Mom asked hopefully.

"Well, no," Dad answered. "Somehow, in the confusion, the big gray leader got away. Now the sheriff has put out word for anyone to shoot him on sight."

"Surely someone will get him soon," Mom replied.

"Yes, I suppose so," said Dad. "But they also found out who that dog belongs to. He is a special kind and very expensive. The owner is all up in the air about it, and he's threatening to get even with anybody who dares to kill him."

"So what now?" asked Mom.

Dad shrugged. "I'd hate to be the one to shoot him.

* * * * * *

Ed Samples, the milk man, was very large and strong, and could swing milk cans onto the truck like they were nothing at all. The next morning Dad talked to him about the big gray dog. Ed said nothing until he was climbing back into his truck. Then he held up one finger and said, "Don't you worry about that dog." He reached behind the seat and Sammie saw him patting the butt of a rifle. Dad winked at him, and Ed slammed the door and drove away smiling.

In the weeks that followed, people kept an eye open for the big gray dog which had caused all the trouble. Whenever people talked about it, Dad just smiled. He knew that no one would ever see him again. And nobody ever did.

Sammie loved to help Dad. As Dad got ready to go to town for the second load of lumber, Sammie asked, " May I go along, Dad?"

Dad looked at him and said, "Run in and ask Mom."

And he ran!

"Mom, may I go with Dad?" he asked running into the kitchen.

"Did you ask Dad?" Mom asked.

"Yes," Sammie said eagerly, "and he said I may if you don't mind."

"Well, go wash your face," Mom replied.

"May I go along, too?" Lydia asked when she heard that Sammie was going.

"No, Lydia, Dad doesn't want to take everybody," Sammie protested.

"Now, now, Sammie," Mom chided.

"Mom, I want to go along, too," Lydia insisted throwing Sammie an annoyed look.

"Well," Mom said then, "Run out and ask Dad."

Sammie hurriedly washed his face and hands and Mom combed his blonde hair straight down. She took his good hat from the hook on the kitchen wall and put it on his head. Sammie had two hats besides his Sunday hat. One was all bent and out of shape. He wore that one to do chores and to work and play around home. This one was the same kind, a yellow straw hat, but it was almost new. He wore it when there was something special going on, and going to town was special. There were two strings on the bottom of the hat which Mom had sewed there. She tied those neatly under his chin and Sammie was ready to go.

"Dad said I may go along, too," Lydia said as she came running back into the house.

So Mom checked her over, too. You had to be clean to go to town. She took down Lydia's black bonnet. Using both hands, she placed it on Lydia's head as straight as could be and tied a neat bow under her chin.

"Okay," Mom said, "Don't keep Dad waiting. Run along now."

And they ran! Dad and Mollie and Dollie and the wagon were waiting in the driveway. They scrambled up over the tailgate into the wagon box and Dad helped them both onto the seat. Sammie sat on one side, Dad sat on the other, and Lydia sat in the middle because she was the smallest.

The seat was high up on the wagon, and they could look down on Mollie and Dollie's broad backs as the horses slowly and steadily trotted away toward town. Dad had a board on which to place his feet, but the children couldn't reach it, so they let their feet dangle.

Town was three and a half miles away. The business district was not very big, but it looked big to the children, because there were so many strange sights to see. They never got tired of looking at all the houses and the stores and the people.

Dad was in a hurry, so he went straight to the lumber yard. He helped the children down from the wagon seat and they went in. Dad talked to the man behind the desk. Sammie couldn't understand all they were saying because they spoke English, but it wasn't boring because there was lots to see.

Then the man came out from behind the counter and patted both of the children gently on the head.

"What are your names?" he asked.

Dad said in German, "Tell him your names."

So Sammie said his name and Lydia said hers. Their voices seemed very small compared to the man's.

He reached under the counter and gave them each a piece of brown candy wrapped in clear paper.

"What do you say now?" Dad asked.

Sammie said "thank you" first and then Lydia did, but again their voices seemed very small.

"Those are root beer barrels," Dad told them on the way home.

The little brown candies did look like barrels and the children couldn't stop looking at them. It was quite tempting to start eating them right away, but they wanted to show the candies to Mom first.

Mom said that it was very nice of that man to give them the candy. Now the children should be kind and unselfish and share with Dannie, because he had stayed home and he didn't have any candy.

"Will that be okay?" she asked.

Sammie wished he didn't have to share. He knew it was naughty to want the candy all for himself when Dannie didn't have any, but he really wanted to say no. He looked at the candy in his hand and then at Mom. Then he said, "Yes, Mom." And Lydia said she would share, too.

"That is nice of you," Mom said.

She took her butcher knife and cut a small chip from each piece. She gave the chips to Dannie and the rest of the candy she handed back to Sammie and Lydia. Taking off the chip had spoiled the shape just a little, but they put the pieces in their mouths and they were delicious! They sucked on them until they were half gone, and then put the rest back into the wrappers to save for the next day.

The new lumber Dad had been bringing in from town was soon going to be made into the lean-to for the calves with the help of neighbors, but before they could come, Dad had to dig out dirt and pour concrete for a foundation. When that was done, they were ready to have a neighborhood frolic.

* * * * * *

Soon after breakfast on the day of the frolic, Orin Graber arrived. He and Dad immediately went to work sawing the lumber to the right lengths.

Sammie loved to watch the fine sawdust drift to the ground and to smell the new lumber. Sammie was fascinated by how smoothly Orin drew the saw back and forth and, not looking where he was walking, stumbled and

went sprawling to the ground right under where Orin was working. Orin stopped sawing so that he wouldn't hit Sammie, laughed and said, "Well, did you catch the mouse?"

Sammie was ashamed. His knee hurt, but he didn't let on.

"You must be more careful," Dad told him.

Sammie quickly got up and stood farther away to watch.

More people came. Uncle Andy brought his whole family. Aunt Lena came to help Mom because it took lots of food to feed the men at a frolic. Cousin Jonas, who was a little older than Sammie, came along and Lydia had

Cousin Sarah to play with. Having someone your own age made the frolic day all the more exciting.

Sammie and Jonas pulled each other on Sammie's wagon for awhile, then they sat and watched the men work. Hammers were banging, and here and there someone was drawing a hand saw back and forth. The work went very fast with all those men there.

The boys then went into the barn and looked at the horses. Uncle Andy always drove fast horses and Jonas was proud of them.

"Our horse is faster than yours," Jonas bragged.

Sammie looked at Uncle Andy's horse and at Queen, but he said nothing. Uncle Andy's horse was black, and Queen was white. Dad always hitched her to the buggy when he wanted to go away. She was a good horse, but right now he wished she was fast, too. He wanted to tell Jonas that Queen was faster, but he knew she wasn't.

"I like black horses better than white!" Jonas declared proudly.

Sammie liked Queen, but he couldn't think of anything to say to defend her. A lump came into his throat. He wanted to say something bad about Uncle Andy's horse, but he couldn't think of anything. He had been very happy that Jonas had come along, but now he began wishing that Jonas had stayed at home.

Sammie heard Mom calling his name, so the boys left the barn and ran to see what she wanted.

"Carry this bench out on the lawn." she requested.

Sammie knew exactly what the bench was for. It was a warm, fall day and the men could wash up in the yard before coming into the house to eat.

Mom gave Sammie and Jonas two basins, some towels and soap which they set on the bench. She then brought a teakettle of hot water from the kitchen and the boys carried a bucket of cold water from the pump in the milkhouse. Now that the washstand was ready, Mom rang the dinnerbell.

The hammers quit pounding and the men came to wash up, visiting all the while.

"The calf business is kind of risky," Sammie heard Eli Mullett say as he dried his hands with a towel. He stole a sideways glance at Dad.

But Dad said nothing.

"It isn't any more risky than raising turkeys," Orin Graber said in his usual jolly manner. A few of the men chuckled. They all knew why he said that. Eli Mullett raised turkeys. Eli's face turned red, but the visiting continued and he soon joined in as before.

Sammie stood thinking. Surely raising calves was a good idea or Dad would not be going into the business.

Mom and Aunt Lena had prepared a large meal and the kitchen was full of good smells. There were bowls of steaming hot mashed potatoes and gravy and fried chicken and dressing and noodles plus the usual applesauce and bread and butter and jelly. For dessert there was a large bowl of graham cracker pudding and canned peaches and cake and Mom's delicious cherry pie.

Sammie's mouth watered as he looked over the table, but he couldn't eat at the first sitting because there wasn't enough room for everyone, and he wasn't company. So he stood and watched as the men got seated. Cousin Jonas was company, so he got to sit next to his father and eat right away. Sammie was sure he had never been so hungry in his life.

After the men had eaten, they went out the door chewing on toothpicks. Mom and Aunt Lena and the girls quickly cleared the table of dirty dishes and reset it. Then, as Sammie and Aunt Lena and the girls and the little children sat down to eat, they could hear hammers once again pounding away. The men were starting on the roof.

By the middle of the afternoon, the lean-to was almost finished. One by one, the men hitched their horses to their buggies and went home. Uncle Andys were the last ones to leave.

Mom came out of the house to see them off. She was carrying Baby David, and Lydia and Dannie came too. The whole family was there to say goodbye.

They watched as Uncle Andy and Dad finished hitching the horse. Then Uncle Andy helped Aunt Lena and the children get into the buggy and climbed in too. The horse arched his neck and pranced eagerly, but Dad held on to his bridle until all was ready.

"Okay," Uncle Andy said, reins in hand and ready to go.

Dad let go and the horse took off.

They all quickly called their goodbyes as the buggy started out the driveway.

"Thanks for your help!" Dad called.

At the road, the horse briefly slowed, while Uncle Andy leaned out and made sure no traffic was coming, then away they went.

Suddenly everything seemed very quiet. All day they had heard the banging of hammers. It had all come to a stop and all they heard now was the distant snappy clop-clopping of Uncle Andys horse.

Dad listened for a little while, and then said, "Come, Sammie."

There were tools to put away and pieces of wood to clean up. Sammie and Lydia loaded wood pieces on the little red wagon and hauled them to the woodshed.

That night after chores and supper they were sitting in the living room. Sammie got his little bench and sat next to Dad's chair.

"Dad," Sammie began.

Dad put his newspaper aside, "What do you want, Sammie?"

"Dad, don't you wish we had a fast horse like Uncle Andy?" Sammie asked.

Dad thought a little then he said, "Queen is safe, Sammie. With a family, I like a safe horse."

Sammie hadn't thought of that. Queen was a safe horse.

"I like a safe horse, too." Sammie said then.

Dad smiled and went back to his reading.

Sammie sat and thought some more. He didn't care if Queen was white. She was a good safe horse. Sometimes Dad even let him drive a little. With a unruly horse he couldn't do that.

Chapter 4
A Busy Time

After the frolic, Dad still had to put in the windows and install the door on the lean-to. Finally he built pens on the inside and the job was finished.

One day soon after, Sammie helped Dad bed the pens. A truck was going to bring calves soon and they had to hurry. Dad carried the silky yellow oat straw from the stack behind the barn with a large fork, and Sammie tore the piles apart and bedded each pen evenly with the straw. When Dad had carried enough, he came and helped. When the calves arrived, they were ready for them.

The calves were black and white and bigger than the ones that were born on the farm last spring. They sniffed at Sammie's hand with their little black noses and tried to suck his fingers.

After milking was done that evening, the calves needed to be fed for the first time. Sammie thought he could give them milk, but Dad smiled a little and shook his head.

"I suppose it will be a man's job," he said.

Sammie was disappointed, but as soon as Dad got started he knew what he had meant. None of the calves had learned to drink from a bucket, and most of them resisted violently.

Dad put the right measure of milk into the bucket, and Sammie held it while Dad caught the first calf. He backed it into a corner and held it there. Next he took the bucket in one hand and stuck the index finger of his other hand into the calf's mouth. As soon as it began sucking, he pushed its head down into the bucket so its mouth was in the milk. The calf jerked up its head and tried to get out of the corner. Next it banged against the side of the pail and milk went flying. Now Dad had to get more milk and try again. After about ten minutes, the first calf was finished and Dad caught another. Already his pant legs were soaked with milk.

Dad kept on until all twenty calves were fed. Sammie watched carefully because, when he was big enough to break calves, he wanted to know how.

"Whew!" Dad said when he was done and they were heading for the house. He looked down over his soaked pant legs. Of course, the first time was the worst. After that it went easier and easier until the calves finally all drank from a pail without a problem.

The corn was ripe and the bottom leaves were already turning brown. Dad strapped a footcutter to his right leg and began cutting corn. He had a bundle of twine, all cut to length, tied to his waist.

The day before, Dad had gone through the fields and made corn bucks. To do that, he had taken two stalks of corn from one row and two from the next and tied them together without cutting them off. That made the beginning of each shock.

Now he walked along the row, cutting a corn stalk with each step and gathering the cut stalks in his arms. When he came to a corn buck, his arms were full of cornstalks. Using a piece of the twine he had fastened around his waist, he tied the armful together to make a bundle and set the bundle against the buck. Then he walked on, cutting and tying another bundle, which then was laid against the next buck. So on he went, up and down the rows until the corn bucks had grown into beautiful corn shocks. He then took longer pieces of twine and tied them around each shock to hold them together, and they were done.

When Dad had cut enough stalks, he began husking the corn that was still standing and flinging it onto the wagon. On the east end of the barn was a lean-to shed, and along its east side was a corn crib. Every day Dad shoveled corn off the wagon into the crib until it was full. By that time all the corn was husked except what was standing on shocks.

It was the last week in October, and most of the leaves had fallen from the trees in the woods. Under the oak tree in the yard was a thick cover of leaves, but here and there on the tree, some brown leaves still clung to the twigs.

One morning Mom said it was Sammie's birthday. She sang the little "Happy Birthday" song as he came downstairs. From now on when people asked how old he was, Sammie had to remember that he was six years old. Being six was quite important, because that meant he'd start school next year.

There was only one thing about his birthday that he didn't like. When Mom or Lydia had a birthday, it was winter and they could make ice cream. But Sammie's birthday came in the fall when there usually was no snow on the ground. Of course Mom always made something special anyway, but nothing was as special as ice cream. The stores in town had ice cream to sell year-'round, and sometimes Dad brought some home for the family, but they couldn't expect store-bought ice cream every time there was a birthday. Dad and Mom said they couldn't afford it.

That day Sammie went with Dad to the corn field to husk corn. The usual way was to tear down two shocks. Dad would then kneel down before a bundle, husk out the ears, and throw them on a pile halfway between where the two original shocks had stood. When all the corn was husked, he gathered the stalks together and made a new

shock — a bigger one — over the pile of husked corn.
During the winter he could come to the field to get corn
for the cows and haul in the corn stalks for feed and
bedding.

But today he needed corn to grind, so he husked onto
the wagon. Sammie stayed on the wagon and held the lines.
When Dad was finished with a shock, he clucked to Mollie
and Dollie, and Sammie guided the horses as they went to
the next shock. There was hardly anything he liked better
than driving the horses for Dad.

The morning was cool and frosty, and before long
Sammie's feet were cold. "Maybe you should get down and
walk around," Dad told him. "That should warm them up."
So he got down off the wagon. Sport was busy sniffing and
finding mice that were hiding under the bundles and
Sammie helped him by kicking bundles and moving them
around.

Suddenly Sammie heard Dad clucking to the horses. He
had wanted to be back on the wagon to do the driving, so
he ran back quickly, but the team had already stopped
when he got there. Sammie climbed on and took the lines,
and decided that, no matter how cold his feet got, he was
not going to get down again! He didn't care if his feet
were cold! Losing a chance to drive the horses was worse
than cold feet.

The sun shone down cheerily and the morning warmed
up. Sammie's feet became warm, and he was comfortable
on the wagon. The pile of corn grew bigger and bigger.
Finally the wagon was full and Dad said it was dinnertime.

Mom had made a good dinner, and in the middle of the
table stood a cake with frosting. On top were six candles!

"There must be something special going on today,"
Dad said when they were seated. He looked at Sammie.

Sammie just grinned.

Then Dad reached out and got a hold on Sammie's ear, "One, two, three, four, five, six, and one to grow on," he counted as he playfully pulled.

When they were ready to eat dessert, Mom took a match and lit the candles on the cake. They all watched them for a short while.

"Now blow them out," Mom said.

And Sammie blew them out all in one big puff.

After that Mom took the candles out and put them back in the box. They would be saved for the next birthday in the family, because little birthday candles were expensive to buy.

After dinner Mom pulled his ear. Next Lydia and Dannie also had their turn. Sammie tried to dodge their playful tugs, but in the end, they all got their pulls in.

"Why do people pull each others' ears on birthdays?" Sammie asked.

"Oh, it is just a way to give some attention to a person who has a birthday," Mom answered. "Do you like having a birthday?"

Sammie nodded.

After dinner, Dad shelled corn which was to be ground into cornmeal. A few days before, he had taken a basket along to the field and, as he husked, he put the nicest ears of corn into the basket. These ears were brought into the house and placed in the oven of Mom's kitchen range, where they had roasted slowly for two days.

Now Dad sat on a kitchen chair with a five gallon bucket between his legs, and shelled the kernels from the cobs.

"Here, Sammie, you can help, too." Dad told him.

He showed Sammie how to hold the ear with one hand and twist it with the other. The kernels easily let loose and went tumbling into the pail. Sammie couldn't shell nearly as fast as Dad, but he could help.

Shelling corn was hard on the hands and it didn't take long for Sammie's hands to become sore.

"Doesn't it hurt your hands?" Sammie asked, stopping and looking at Dad.

"Oh, they get a little sore. But look here," Dad pointed to the basket, "we're almost done."

So Sammie kept on. He liked the nutty smell of the toasted corn. He looked into the pail. A few of the kernels were deep dark brown, some were pale brown, but many of them were as yellow as they had been in the field.

When the shelling was done, Dad took the corn outside to "put it through the wind", as it was called. He lifted the pail of corn as high as he could reach and slowly poured it into another pail standing on the ground. The kernels were heavy and fell straight down, but the chaff and the light kernels were picked up by the wind and taken away. He poured them back and forth three times, and, in the end, he had a pail of beautiful, clean kernels all ready to be made into cornmeal.

In the afternoon when Dad went to town to have feed ground for the cows, he took the toasted corn along. The mill ground it into good, fine cornmeal.

That evening for supper they had cornmeal mush. They poured milk over it and added a little butter to enhance the flavor. After they had eaten, there was still plenty of mush left. Mom scraped the extra into a cake pan and set it in the washhouse to cool.

The next morning it had hardened enough to be sliced and fried in little pieces. Sammie loved fried cornmeal mush topped with Mom's delicious tomato gravy. He ate until he was full, and then washed the mush down with a glass of good cold milk.

Winter was coming, and Dad had lots of work to do. Corn husking took a lot of his time. One day he hauled a load of coal from town with the wagon. The next day he went to the feed mill and brought home a load of corn cobs. For days, he and Orin Graber's son, Allen, took the crosscut saw and sawed wood poles in the woods to the south. Every evening he came driving home with a load. When there was a big enough pile of poles in the yard, Orin brought his buzz saw and they cut them up for firewood.

"That saw is dangerous," Dad told Sammie. Sawing poles was one job Sammie could not help with. He just had to stand back a good distance and watch.

When the cutting was done, Dad split the chunks. If they split easily, he used his ax. But the large tough pieces were harder. He started a large steel wedge into the wood, and then, using a maul, pounded on the wedge until the pieces were forced apart.

Sammie could help carry the wood into the woodshed and stack it. The small pieces which went into the kitchen range were stacked on one side, and the large chunks for the living room heater went on the other.

"Now let the cold wind blow," Dad said when they were done. There was enough fuel in the woodshed to last the winter. Mom could use the corn cobs and the smaller wood pieces in the kitchen. The living room heater would be kept going with coal and large wood chunks.

Sammie filled the wood box behind the living room heater and Dad brought in the coal because it was so heavy. Loading up the wood box next to the kitchen range was a job for both Sammie and Lydia. It was hard work to keep fuel in the house, but that was what kept the house nice and warm, so the children should be glad to help. Dad and Mom said so.

The little farm lay ready for winter. The large yellow strawstack stood over a frame of posts and boards, making a cozy place for the heifers to sleep and providing plenty of straw for bedding inside the barn. The corncrib was full and there were piles of corn under the shocks in the cornfield. There were plenty of oats to feed the horses and the mow was full of hay.

All summer long Mom had canned hundreds of jars of vegetables and fruits. There were potatoes and apples and carrots and cabbage and pumpkins in the root cellar. While they didn't have much money, they did have everything they and their animals needed to be well fed and comfortable when the cold winds blew. Mom said they had much to be thankful for.

Thanksgiving Day wasn't far away and Mom planned to invite company. The children wanted to know who was coming, but she just smiled and tantalized them by saying, "Oh, you'll find out soon enough."

No matter how much they coaxed, Mom would not tell. When they asked Dad, he only smiled.

Chapter 5

Thanksgiving

One morning Mom said the children had to be good and help her because she was preparing for company. Tomorrow was Thanksgiving Day and the house had to be cleaned from top to bottom. Mom washed the windows and the woodwork. Lydia helped by sweeping the floors so Mom could get started with the mopping sooner. After dinner Mom asked Sammie to help Lydia with the dishes.

"That way I can go on with the cleaning and preparing food," she told them.

So they rolled up their sleeves and Lydia stood on a little a bench and began washing dishes. Sammie didn't like to do dishes, but he took a dish towel and slowly started drying them.

"This is girls' work," he told Lydia, "It seems I always have to help you with your work, but you don't have to help with mine."

"That's not true!" Lydia retorted, "I do too help you with yours!"

"Well, I have lots more work than you do," Sammie said.

"You don't either!" Lydia insisted. " I do a whole pile of things. I sweep floors and wash dishes and rock Baby David and...."

"Now, now children," Mom cut in, "Don't argue. Why don't you trade for a day? Maybe that would help you to be more happy with your own work."

"Yes, let's trade," Sammie said eagerly nodding his head.

"Okay," Lydia said, not too sure that she wanted to.

"Why don't you trade today? After dishes are done, Lydia may go out and help Dad, and Sammie can stay inside and be my helper," Mom said.

At first Sammie was happy with the arrangement. Mom didn't have a whole lot for him to do, so he had time to play. But in the middle of the afternoon, Dad hitched Queen up to the buggy and went to Eli Mullets' and Lydia and Dannie got to go along. Already Sammie wished he had not traded work with Lydia, for he knew that if he had been out helping Dad, he would have been allowed to go.

When Dad and the children came home, they brought three half-grown kittens which Eli Mullett had given them. They were happy to have them, because they didn't have many cats now. Some of the ones which had been on the farm had gotten sick and died, and one had been killed on the road. The only cat left was a wild tomcat, and the children couldn't play with him.

Sammie ran out to look at the little kittens. One was a yellow tiger, one was black with a white neck and chin, and the other was gray all over. But Sammie was only allowed to look at them for a minute before going back into the house to help Mom. Lydia and Dannie got to stay in the barn and make a bed for the kittens.

By that time he was quite tired of staying in the house.

"Mom, may I go out and do my chores and have Lydia come back in?" he asked.

"No, Sammie, you know what the deal is. You were sure Lydia didn't work as much as you do, and you were quite eager to trade. Now you shall stick to it until the day is over," Mom answered. Sammie knew that begging would do no good.

After supper Lydia got to sit in the living room with Dad while Sammie helped Mom do the dishes. Usually it was the other way around.

Sammie stood thinking as he slowly wiped the dishes. He was going to be more careful what he said about Lydia's work. Maybe she didn't work as hard, but rocking Baby David and wiping dishes and dusting furniture took patience. And he just couldn't stand being cooped up in the house. Sammie was very glad when that day was over.

The next morning was Thanksgiving Day. When Sammie and Dad came in from chores, good smells were already coming from Mom's kitchen. The day before, Mrs. Mullet had sent them a turkey all dressed and ready for the pan. The Mullets' turkeys had done well and they had saved one on purpose for the Thanksgiving dinner. Now it was roasting in the oven.

There were pumpkin pies in the pantry and bowls of pudding on the windowsill in the washhouse. On the washing machine lid stood a large bowl of shredded carrots fixed in orange jello, and on the cabinet in the kitchen stood a pan of toasted bread crumbs to be used for dressing. And Mom was still busy. There were potatoes to peel and noodles to cook. Cans of fruit had to be brought from the root cellar, and the little children had to be helped into their Sunday clothes.

"Hurry up, Sammie!" Mom said when he was halfway through eating his breakfast. She hurried up Lydia when she was wiping dishes and she hurried up Sammie when he was changing clothes. And all morning she also hurried.

Dad helped, too. He helped Dannie into his clothes, and he emptied the slop bucket. Finally they were almost ready. Sammie and Lydia had just finished setting the table when they heard the sound of horses. The children still didn't know who was coming.

Sammie ran to the window. Uncle Andys were coming down the highway in their surrey to which they had two horses hitched. They turned in at the driveway and stopped by the house. Sammie grabbed his cap and coat and ran outside. On the front seat with Uncle Andy sat Grandfather! He and Uncle Andy both held one of the little cousins, and Jonas sat in between. In the back seat sat Aunt Lena and Grandmother with the little girls and the baby. It was quite a load.

What a surprise! Grandfather and Grandmother had come on the train all the way from Tennessee to be with them on Thanksgiving Day! As Dad helped Uncle Andy with the horses, more buggies began arriving because, of course, all the other aunts and uncles and cousins who lived nearby wanted to spend Thanksgiving with Grandfather and Grandmother, too.

Dad and the other men went into the house to visit, but the boys stayed in the barn. They walked behind the horses and talked about them. Each boy thought his father's horses were the best.

"Our horses are the fastest," Cousin Jonas said proudly as they admired Uncle Andys team.

"You can't drive your horses, because they are too wild. Dad lets me drive Queen sometimes," Sammie said wisely.

"When I'm older, I can drive them," Jonas retorted, "I wouldn't want a white horse and Queen would be much too slow for me."

Sammie didn't like what Jonas said. Queen was a good safe horse. He wished Jonas would agree to that, but he didn't. To get the boys away from the horses, Sammie showed them the little kittens, but Jonas didn't think they were anything special.

"We have more just like them at home," he said.

"Let's go up to the haymow," Sammie said. He scrambled up the ladder and the other boys followed.

All forenoon they played in the mow until they heard Dad calling that it was dinner time. Then, down the ladder they went.

"Let's race!" Jonas yelled, and they ran for the house.

He was the biggest, so of course he won. But Sammie was next. They came puffing into the kitchen all red-faced from the cold and exercise, took off their wraps, and lined up to wash their hands and faces. For the first time they realized they were hungry. Good smells came from the food spread out over the table.

Dad and Grandfather and the other men were already at the table. The boys filled up the bench against the wall. But, as on the day of the frolic, there wasn't enough room. Sammie wasn't company, so again he had to wait. Now he was really hungry! He went to the living room and sat down. He could hear the knives and forks and spoons rattle as the others ate the good roast turkey and mashed potatoes and gravy and dressing and all the other things. He felt hollow inside, and it took a long time for the others to eat. But finally all was quiet as they gave thanks and they were done.

Right away the other boys ran back outside. The men went to the living room and the ladies hurried to reset the table. Then Sammie sat down at the table with Mom and Aunt Lena and the girls and ate.

The food was good, but Sammie couldn't forget that the other boys were outside playing already. As soon as he was allowed, he ran outside to join them.

When he came to the barn, the other boys were playing in the feed room. They were giving feed to the calves and spreading feed on the floor. Sammie knew that Dad would never allow him to play in the feed or waste any, and he knew that he should tell the boys to stop. But what would the boys say? Maybe Jonas would make fun of him. Maybe the other boys were allowed to play like that at their home. In the end, Sammie joined in and played in the feed also.

Then, in the late afternoon, the company left as suddenly as they had come, except for Grandfather and Grandmother. They were going to stay for a few days before going back to their home in Tennessee.

The sun was low in the western sky, reminding them all that it was chore time. Dad and Sammie and Mom and Grandfather changed into everyday clothes and went to the barn.

"Sammie, what do you know about this?" Dad said as he came out of the feed room shaking his head, "What a mess, I-yi-yi-yi!" he looked at Mom and went on, "There's chicken feed, calf feed, and cow feed scattered all over!"

Sammie hung his head. Why had he done it? He felt terrible! He didn't want to tell Dad what had happened. But Dad kept asking questions until Sammie had told him the whole story.

"You say the other boys started it, but I still can't let you off. You need to learn to mind what I say!" Dad said. Sammie knew he had to take what was coming. Dad's whippings hurt and, with Grandfather there, it made it all the worse.

When the punishment was over, he felt better. The rest of the evening Dad was soft-spoken and kind. Sammie knew that Dad hated to punish him, but he had to learn to obey.

While Dad milked the last cow, Grandfather sat on a milk stool nearby. He reached out and pulled Sammie toward him. "Sometimes it is hard to be good, Sammie, but if you obey your father, you will never be sorry," Grandfather said softly.

Sammie leaned against Grandfather's knee. He felt much happier. He could feel that Grandfather cared. From now on he would try to mind what Dad said.

Chapter 6

Shipping Fever

After Thanksgiving the weather gradually grew colder. The wind felt sharper, the ground froze hard, and the world wore a dreary look. The woods were black and the weeds and the grasses along the road and the fence rows were a dull brown. All the summer colors were gone. Almost all the leaves had fallen from the big oak tree and had blown away.

Every day Dad and Sammie fed the calves in the lean-to. It was no longer necessary to give them milk. They ate ground feed like the cows, and Dad said it was time to sell them. So a truck came and took them away. Dad was happy. The calves had grown well and the price was good.

One day the sky was gray and the air was cold and damp. "The wind's from the east," Dad said when he came in from chores that evening, "We'll see other weather or I'll miss my guess." The next morning the ground was white with snow. It lay clean and fresh all over the farm. The only thing that broke the snowy cover was the places where the snowplows had gone up and down the highway and the path to the barn.

When Sammie went to the barn, the snow had quit falling, but the wind was picking up now and carrying the snow away. Snow came whirling around the edge of the buildings and dropped in drifts here and there.

Sammie shivered and drew in his shoulders. He was warmly dressed in his winter clothes, but the wind chilled him anyway. However, inside the barn all was cozy and warm. The wind and snow could not get at the animals penned up inside. They all stood contentedly eating the feed which Dad had put in front of them and blowing billows of steam into the air as they breathed. Even the little calves blew little billows and looked eagerly at Sammie for feed.

The two lanterns hanging from nails in the beams cast a light so Dad and Mom could see to do their milking, and so that Sammie could feed the calves and give them water. When Sammie finished with the calves, he went to water the horses. Of all the animals, he liked them best. When he came close, Queen looked at him with her soft eyes and stretched toward him sniffing with her pink nose. But he couldn't give her any feed, because Dad did that first thing when he came to the barn. Now the horses had eaten and were ready to drink. One by one he slipped off their halters and let them go to the trough for a drink --- first Queen, and then Mollie, and then Dollie. When they had finished drinking, they came back into their stalls, and Sammie climbed onto the manger and put their halters back on.

On the very end of the horse stalls stood Tim, the all-purpose horse. Sammie didn't go in beside him. "I don't want you to get hurt," Dad said from time to time. When people came close, Tim laid back his ears and snapped. He did not like people. But Dad had worked with Tim and he did not snap at Dad. Dad said Tim was a one-man horse. While Sammie let Queen and Mollie and Dollie go for water, Tim pawed the ground impatiently. When Sammie went into Dollie's stall, which was right next to Tim's, Tim laid back his ears and looked angry. So Tim had to wait until Dad had time to lead him to water.

After breakfast, Dad hitched Mollie and Dollie to the wagon and went to the cornfield to get a load of corn.

Sammie and Lydia bundled up in their winter wraps and went out to play in the snow. Soon Dad came driving up with his load of corn, and stopped by the barn.

"Come with me, Sammie," he called as he jumped from the wagon.

Sammie followed him into the barn to get some burlap feed sacks. Dad picked up the scoop shovel and they went to the little granary southwest of the barn. Sammie held the sacks while Dad filled them with oats.

"Hold the sack tightly in the back and let the front hang loose," Dad told Sammie. Then Dad shoveled oats into the bag until it was full. After it was filled, Dad tied the top shut, then hefted the sack of oats up to his shoulder and carried it to the wagon, where he pitched it on top of the load of corn. He then came back, and they began filling the next sack, and so on until they had enough sacks filled. When they were done, Dad was ready to go to the mill to get feed ground for the cows.

"May I go along?" Sammie asked.

Dad looked at him, "Your clothes are wet from playing in the snow, and you are shivering already. I think you had better go to the house and dry out."

Sammie was disappointed, but he looked down over his clothes. They were wet and his toes were getting cold. He looked at Lydia. Her clothes were wet, too, and she was shivering.

"Will you get us some candy?" Sammie asked then.

"Candy!" Dad teased, "What do you want with candy?"

"We want to eat it," Sammie answered.

"Yes, we want candy," Lydia joined in.

Dad climbed up on the wagon and looked down at them.

"I suppose the more you get, the more you want. Don't you think so?" Dad said smiling just a little.

The children didn't say any more. They stood there and watched as Mollie and Dollie pulled the wagon out the driveway and onto the road. The wheels made wide tracks in the unbroken snow. On the roadway the snowplows had plowed away all the snow except a thin layer which was smooth and hard from all the traffic that had driven over it. The large wagon wheels rolled quietly over the hard packed, snowy road, and the horses trotted away toward town with Dad sitting up high on the oat sacks.

"He never gets us any candy," Lydia said dejectedly as they started walking toward the house.

"I know," Sammie agreed. Maybe Dad would bring some, but he doubted it. What Dad had said was that if he'd get them candy, they'd just want more.

It was almost noon when Dad came driving home. Sammie ran out and followed him as he unloaded the feed. He looked all over, but he could see only feed on the wagon.

"He didn't get any candy," Sammie told Lydia when he came into the house.

"I knew he wouldn't," Lydia answered quietly.

Dad came in and stood inside the door looking at the children. Then he laughed and reached into his coat pocket. Out came a bag of candy!

The children looked a little sheepish, but not for long. Candy was a real treat!

Dad had brought home corn candy. After dinner Mom counted out five pieces for each of the children, closed the bag, and put it in the cabinet.

"We'll put this away for later," she said.

The next day a truck brought some more calves, but this bunch was not like the first. Three days later one was sick and wouldn't eat. Dad gave it some medicine and put it in a pen by itself. By evening two more were sick, and the next morning, another.

It was a fast disease. By that evening, the calf that had become sick first was dead. By the next morning, some more were sick. Dad quietly ate his breakfast and went out. He didn't whistle and he didn't talk much. At noon he came in and sat quietly eating his dinner.

"What do you think is wrong with them?" Mom asked.

Dad shook his head, "Beats me, I've never seen anything like it. They don't respond to any medicine I give."

"Maybe you should get the vet." Mom suggested.

Dad shrugged and said no more.

After dinner Sammie followed Dad to the lean-to. Most of the calves stood with their backs hunched up and their eyes were dull and black. They paid no attention to Sammie, no matter how close he came to them. He stood looking at them. Maybe this was what Eli Mullet had meant when he had said that calves were a risky business.

"I'm going to call the vet," Dad said after looking the calves over again.

"May I go along, too?" Sammie asked.

"No, just stay here," Dad said.

So Sammie went outside and watched as Dad walked down the road to the Gressingers' to call the veterinarian.

The vet came late that afternoon. "Shipping fever" is what he called that disease. He gave shots and left some medicine to be given later.

"Call me if they don't get better," he said climbing into his car.

"Okay, and thanks," Dad said.

"Okie-dokie," the vet responded, and he drove away.

By the next day some more calves had died, but a few others were better. Dad gave them all medicine and fed the ones that ate. Gradually they kept getting better until there were no more sick ones. But over half of them had died. Sammie could count all the calves that were left, and there were nine. Dad said those probably wouldn't grow as well now because they were stunted by the disease.

Sammie heard Dad and Mom talking. Dad said there was bound to be a loss on this bunch of calves. The lean-to was not paid for yet. It was going to take good management to pay all the bills, and there wouldn't be much money left for groceries.

But Mom said, "Oh, we'll make do. We'll just eat more corn meal mush, and we have plenty of milk and butter. Soon we'll be butchering, and that will give us plenty of beef and pork, plus we have ten young roosters left from last summer. As long as the chickens don't molt, we'll have eggs. We'll make more rivvel soup, plus we have vegetables in the root cellar, not to mention the fruit. We should be able to get by without buying much."

"I guess it will work out somehow," Dad said.

One day Mom sent Sammie and Lydia to the root cellar to get a can of sweet corn. She opened it and made a wry face. It was spoiled.

"Go get another jar, please," she told them.

The next jar was spoiled too. Later that day Mom and Dad went to the root cellar to check the corn. Every jar was spoiled and they poured them out.

"Well, we can't count on those now," Dad said.

"No," Mom answered, "But we'll make do anyhow."

Christmas wasn't very far away. Several times Sammie heard Dad and Mom talking about it, but when he came close, they stopped.

He thought and thought. If there was no money for groceries, there would be no money for Christmas presents. That was easy to figure out.

Mom said they were going to Uncle Andys' for Christmas dinner. Sammie was happy to think about being with the uncles and aunts and cousins for Christmas. But one thing bothered him. What if the cousins all got Christmas presents, and Dad and Mom couldn't afford to buy any. He could hardly bear that thought!

Sammie thought about the spoiled sweet corn every now and then for the rest of the day, and was still thinking about it that night when they were all sitting in the living room.

"Mom," Sammie began.

"Yes, Sammie, what do you want?" Mom responded.

"Mom, why did all the sweet corn spoil?" he asked.

"Well, maybe we weren't careful enough when we canned it," Mom explained. "The jars have to be clean and sterile, and they have to be cold-packed long enough so that any germs that are still in the corn are killed. Even if we are careful and do everything right, these things sometimes happen."

"Will we have enough things to eat for winter?" Sammie asked then. He was still thinking about Christmas, but didn't want to say it.

"Don't worry, Sammie. Everything will be okay," Mom assured him.

Sammie said no more, but he still wondered.

Chapter 7

Rooster Sale

Mom got an idea for making a little extra money. There were still ten roosters left from last summer. They had been counting on them for table meat, but the weather was cold now and butchering time was just around the corner. After that they would have plenty of beef and pork. Mom decided to butcher the roosters and take the dressed fryers to town to sell.

"I think we can make do without the roosters," Mom told Dad.

"Well, whatever you think." Dad said.

So one morning Sammie and Lydia carried in extra wood from the woodshed, and Mom built a fire under the large iron kettle in the washhouse. When the water was steaming, she said, "Run out and tell Dad the water is hot."

Next to the small chicken house was a chopping block. Dad caught two roosters and handed them to Sammie. He caught one more and gave it to Lydia. Then he caught another which he took to the chopping block.

The children wished they could run to the house until the job was done. But Dad wanted them to stay and hold roosters for him. So both of them turned away long enough for Dad to bring down his ax on the chopping block. Dad's stroke was swift and sure and one by one all ten of the roosters were killed.

Next Dad and the children picked the feathers. Dad dipped each of the dead roosters into a bucket of hot water until it was scalded just right. Dad knew just how long to leave them in so that the feathers came out easily, but not so long that the skin would come off, too.

When the roosters were picked "clean as a whistle," Sammie carried them into the washhouse where Mom took out the insides and dressed them ready for market. By noon ten dressed fryers lay in a neat row on the butchering table.

For dinner Mom rolled the chicken livers in flour and fried them in her large iron skillet. The family could eat those, because the people in town who bought the dressed fryers didn't care for them. Dinner was home-fried potatoes with gravy, chicken livers rolled in flour and fried in homemade butter, plus green beans and canned peaches for dessert. After the noon meal was finished, Dad hitched Queen to the buggy and brought it to the door. Mom put the dressed fryers in bags and loaded them on the buggy, because she was going into town to sell the fryers.

"May I go along?" Sammie asked.

"No, Sammie," Mom answered. "You may stay in the house with the little children this afternoon. Every once in a while Dad will come in and check on things, but I need you to be the babysitter this afternoon."

So Sammie had to stay in the house with the other children. He and Lydia and Dannie could play games, but the minute Baby David woke up or began fussing, he had to stop playing and rock him. Every little while Dad came in to see if all was okay, and to tend to Baby David's needs.

The arrangement worked just fine, but Sammie got tired of staying in the house. The afternoon seemed very long. He looked out the window and wished he could go out, but Dad and Mom had told him to stay inside, and he knew he had to. Complaining was no use. Although Sammie got lonesome staying in the house, he knew he was helping out. He was happy that they had found a way to make a little extra "grocery money," as Mom had put it.

Finally, he saw Queen and the buggy coming down the highway, and soon Mom was home.

Sammie grabbed his cap and coat and quickly pulled on his overshoes. He ran out just as Mom stopped by the house. He was very eager to see what Mom had bought, but she said, "Hold Queen while I unload my things, Sammie." Sammie went to Queen's head and held on to her bridle. Dad came from the barn.

"Did the fryers sell okay?" Dad asked.

"Yes, I could easily have sold more," Mom said happily. Dad took Queen by the bridle and led her to the barn. Sammie started to follow Mom to the house. Then Dad turned and said. "It is chore time, Sammie." So Sammie turned around and went with Dad to the barn. It was nice to be allowed to go outside again, but Sammie really wondered what all Mom had bought in town.

Chapter 8

Christmas

On Christmas morning it was cold. Sammie shivered as he crawled out of his warm bed, grabbed his clothes, and hurried downstairs. Dad had fired up the living room heater, but the house was still very chilly, and Sammie's teeth chattered in the cold. He knew that the one place which was sure to be warm on cold mornings was behind the kitchen stove, and that is where he went. He could sit on the woodbox in the stove's friendly warmth and slowly get dressed. Now and then he'd doze off where he was sitting, and then Mom would say, "Get dressed, Sammie, it is time to go to the barn."

How he hated to leave that toasty warm place. But chores had to be done, and Mom was ready to get started on them. Dad was already out in the barn.

Outside all was dark and cold and still. No wind was blowing. Millions of tiny stars glittered in the clear sky. They seemed to be trying to pierce the frosty cold, but it made no difference. The cold was so intense that nothing could stop it.

It felt good to get inside the warm barn. Now Sammie was wide awake. It was Christmas morning! Dad and Mom had often told the children that Christmas morning was the birthday of Jesus. It was more important to think about the Savior lying in a manger than about presents and candy and things. But Sammie wished he had looked around a bit before coming to the barn. Maybe, just maybe, there were presents waiting for him.

All the animals had to be cared for before they could go back to the house. Sammie hurried to give the little calves their milk and to feed the bigger ones. The animals all stood eating their feed like normal. They paid no attention to special days. They were snug and cozy in the warm barn, with plenty of feed and water in front of them. That was the kind of Christmas that animals liked.

When the chores were finished, they returned to the house. Sammie looked around, but couldn't see any presents. They ate breakfast as usual. After breakfast was over, Mom said, "As soon as the dishes are done, I'll see if I can find some presents. Who all wants to help?'

Both Sammie and Lydia said quickly, "I do!"

Even Dannie noticed their excitement and said, "Me too!" but he was too small to reach the sink, so he couldn't help much.

Sammie and Lydia usually had trouble keeping up when Mom washed the dishes, but not this morning. Each time she put a piece in the drainer, they quickly grabbed it and dried it, and they were done in record time.

Then Mom brought the presents from the bedroom. There were two little packages almost the same size. The other two were large. One was square and one oblong. They were all wrapped in clean white paper.

Sammie looked at the big long package. It was the right size and shape to hold a toy semi-truck. He often listened as real trucks came down Highway 22. They always slowed down for the curve, then with a mighty roar they shifted gears and went on. How he wished for a toy truck! He sometimes used pieces of wood to play truck in the driveway, but a real toy truck would be so much better.

When Mom set the long package in front of Lydia, Sammie couldn't believe it! He had been so sure it held a truck for him. Instead he got one of the smallest packages.

He tried to hide his disappointment as he began opening it. Then out came a little wagon with toy horses hitched to it. In a minute he forgot all about trucks. The wagon was red with yellow wheels and the horses were brown. What more could any boy want? He was so excited, he hardly noticed what the others had.

Lydia had a box of toy dishes and Dannie had a beautiful musical top. Baby David's package contained a big plastic rattle in the shape of a safety pin. Dad helped Dannie with his top. When he made it spin really fast, it hummed a pleasing tune.

"Have you forgotten your manners, children?" Dad asked then.

Sammie looked up. Mom was smiling at him.

"Thank you!" he quickly said.

Then the other children said their "thank you's." That is, all except Baby David. He was too small to say anything. He just banged the new rattle against the arm of the rocking chair and was happy to be safely in Mom's lap.

Suddenly Mom looked at the clock. "My, my! We must hurry!" she exclaimed. She jumped up from her chair and put Baby David on the floor. "Children," she said, "you may put your things away now. We must hurry to get ready to go to Uncle Andys'."

"May I take this along?" Sammie asked, holding up his horses and wagon.

Mom shook her head, "Put it away now, Sammie."

He carefully placed it on Mom's bureau where the little ones couldn't reach it and went to get ready.

They all quickly dressed in their Sunday best and bundled up for the cold. Dad brought Queen and the buggy to the door, and they got on. Sammie and Lydia sat on a low seat at Dad and Mom's feet. Dad held Dannie, and Baby David sat on Mom's lap all bundled up from head to toe. Even his face was covered with a thin piece of cloth, leaving just enough space so he could still see out. But he didn't like being covered up, and cried until the buggy began moving.

Dad tucked in the blankets and snapped the oil cloth into place over the door and front openings. Now the children couldn't see out, but Sammie knew where they were going. The steel tires screeched as they rolled over the cold snow. When they reached the road, the screeching stopped because the road was bare. The sound was replaced by the steady rumble of the buggy wheels and Queen's clop-clop on the hard road surface.

The oil cloth was snapped so high in the front that only Dad could peek out. Mom could see out if she stretched, but none of the children could. The driving lines came in through a slit, and Dad held them steadily with his large gloved hands. Everyone was cozy and warm behind the oil cloth and under the blankets for the two-mile trip to Uncle Andys'.

Uncle Andys' children had received a brand new sled. It was a nice sled, but Sammie knew he wouldn't trade his horses and wagon for it. Jonas stepped inside the rope which was attached to both ends of the handle. Sammie tied some twine around Jonas' waist and sat on the sled. Then he drove Jonas up and down the icy driveway like a horse.

Next it was Sammie's turn to be the horse. Jonas drove him for a while, then guided him to the rear wheel of Dad's buggy. He tied him up there and walked away.

Sammie did his best to act like a horse. He stamped his feet and tossed his head. He moved his mouth like a horse champing at the bit. The steel tire was shiny and clean in front of him. He leaned forward and licked it, because it seemed like something a horse might do. But then a terrible thing happened! The tire was cold and his tongue instantly froze to it! It stung! He pulled back in a hurry! Oooh! It came loose, but it hurt!

He took off his mitten and felt his tongue. It was still all there, but it was bleeding. What had he done! He could see a layer of skin on the tire where he had licked.

Sammie forgot all about playing horse or about being a big boy. He cried. "What's wrong?" Jonas asked running toward him. He took one look and ran to the house.

Dad came out right away and looked at Sammie's tongue.

"Don't cry, Sammie," Dad said, "It just took off the skin. It will heal again."

He stopped crying, but he felt terrible. Why had he done it? Now all the aunts and uncles and cousins would know how stupid he had been.

Dad wiped Sammie's tears with his handkerchief. By now more cousins had come and Jonas went on playing with them. But Sammie didn't feel like playing. He followed Dad to the house.

"He licked a cold steel buggy tire," Dad explained to Mom when they were inside.

Sammie was embarrassed. How silly that sounded! Mom took a look at his tongue and said it would be all right. The grownups were laughing and talking about it. Sammie wished he were somewhere else, but he sat on a little chair next to Dad's and said nothing.

"It will heal again," Uncle Andy told him, "I did the same thing when I was a boy. I had to learn the hard way, too."

Sammie felt a little better now. At least he wasn't the only person who had done something like that. He still didn't feel like playing, however, and stayed inside until dinner time.

Of course Aunt Lena had all kinds of good things on the table for the Christmas dinner, and Sammie was company so he got to eat at the first setting. But his tongue hurt and his stomach didn't feel the best, so he didn't eat much.

After dinner the other boys wanted Sammie to come out to play. He went out but he didn't feel much like playing.

"You should have known better," one of the boys told him, "My father once told me what happens when you lick cold steel."

"Well, nobody ever told me," Sammie defended himself.

"Nobody ever told me either," Cousin Jonas said, siding with Sammie.

It felt good to have somebody sticking up for him. No more was said about it and they played all afternoon.

Later as Queen clop-clopped toward home, Sammie sat thinking and feeling sorry for himself. His day had really been spoiled. But then he remembered his toy horses and wagon, and by the time they arrived home, he was much happier. He ran right into the house and began playing. When Mom saw him she said, "Put the toys away, Sammie, and go change your clothes. It is chore time."

He fingered the horses and wagon a minute longer, and then put them back on the bureau. He would hurry with his chores and play afterwards.

The next morning his tongue felt better, and in a few days it was healed. For a long time he could clearly imagine the sting when he thought about it. He never forgot the lesson he learned about licking steel in cold weather.

Chapter 9

Butchering Day

On the day after Christmas, Dad said it was time for butchering. The weather was still cold, but not bitter. During the day the sun warmed the snow and it became heavy and wet. At night it got cold again, and the mornings were crisp. It was just right for "hanging up a beef".

Dad killed a steer and began skinning it. He set the ladder up against the rafter of the lean-to shed, fastened a good sturdy chain to the rafter, and hung a block and tackle from it. He hooked the bottom end of the block and tackle to the center ring of the single-tree which was fastened to the hind legs of the carcass, and pulled the carcass up toward the rafter. When the carcass was off the ground, he made a long cut down the center of the belly from the hind legs to the front legs and removed the insides. Then he continued with the skinning. Finally the skin was off, and the carcass of clean red beef, with streaks of white tallow and sinew, hung from the rafter.

The last thing he had to do was divide the carcass into halves. Dad took his sharp ax and chopped down through the middle of the backbone. Then he pulled the sides of meat up as far as they would go so that neither Sport nor a stray dog nor a wild animal could get at it. There they left them to hang for a whole week. Hanging made beef more tender and better to eat.

Dad and Mom helped back and forth with Orin Graber's at butchering time. The Grabers had five children.

Allen was a grown boy and he sometimes worked for Dad. Next came the twelve-year-old twin girls, Elsie and Ella. Freeman was next and Abner was the youngest.

Abner wasn't much bigger than Sammie, but they never played together much. Abner was usually with Freeman, and Sammie was afraid of Freeman. Once when he was at the Graber home, Freeman had grabbed Sammie and threatened to throw him into the water tank. He hadn't done it, but Sammie had often seen Freeman throw cats and chickens into the tank, so he didn't trust him. Freeman knew Sammie was scared of him, so he teased Sammie all the more.

On butchering day the whole Graber family came. Orin brought his knives and pig scrapers and Mrs. Graber brought large bowls and more knives and extra aprons for herself and the girls.

Dad had gotten the scalding trough ready the day before and that morning had tied the pig, still alive and grunting, by a hind leg to the corner of the shed near where the sides of beef were hanging. Everything was ready.

Orin began sharpening knives the minute he arrived. Sammie and Lydia loved to watch. With the sharpening steel in one hand and the knife in the other, Orin drew the knife back and forth so fast that the children couldn't see it go. He sharpened all the knives and laid them in a neat row on a board close to the place they were going to work.

The children had to stay away from the knives because they were so sharp. Dad's rifle was propped up against the corncrib, and they had to stay away from that, too.

Before they began butchering, Orin told them a little story. He looked at Dad and said, "Better watch out so it doesn't go like the man who wanted to butcher six hogs at once. It was back in the days when they had muzzle loaders. Those were guns that had to be loaded through the barrel using a ramrod," Orin explained, "You put the powder in first, then pushed the bullet down to make it ready to shoot."

"Well, this guy wanted to butcher six hogs, so he decided to put six loads into the gun at once. He thought he would shoot all six hogs one after another without having to reload."

"But, it didn't work that way. Of course, when he went to shoot the first hog, all six of the loads went off at the same time with an enormous KER-BOOOOM! that knocked him flat on his back." Now Orin was laughing so hard that he could hardly go on with the story.

"Another guy walked up before this guy got to his feet and wanted to pick up the muzzle loader," Orin laughed some more and went on, "That guy struggled to sit up and told him to leave that thing be! 'There's five shots left in it, yet!' he said."

Dad and Orin both laughed about the joke and got on with the work, but Sammie, not understanding much about these things at only 6 years old, wasn't sure exactly why they were laughing.

Dad picked up his rifle to kill the pig, and the children ran quickly to the washhouse and stayed inside until they heard the shot. Killing the animal was the only part of butchering they didn't like. The rest of the day was fun. When they came back out, Orin was cutting a slit in the dead pig's throat so it would bleed out.

Dad had told Sammie to stay nearby. When the men needed something from the house or barn, he could run and get it. Orin told Freeman and Abner to stay there, too, but they didn't. As soon as Orin got busy and didn't notice, they took off for the barn on the run.

All morning they stayed in the barn. Once when Sammie went there for some twine, he saw what they were doing. The little yellow tiger kitten was crouched on a beam by the cow stable. Freeman was poking at it with a hay fork and finally managed to push the frightened little thing off. It fell to the ground and took off running with Freeman and Abner close behind. Quickly it scrambled up a post and again crouched on a beam at the far end of the barn. Again they poked at it with the fork while the kitten hissed and spat and clawed trying to scare them off.

Sammie felt sorry for the kitten, but he didn't dare say anything. He got the twine and went back where the men were working.

A little later he saw Freeman and Abner out in the barnyard. Freeman had a hold on Mollie's tail. He braced his feet and let her pull him across the snowy barnyard. Next Abner did the same thing with Dollie.

Dad looked at the barnyard and said, a little under his breath, "I hope they don't try that with Tim. He'd probably kick the daylights out of them."

Sammie looked at Orin working on the pig. He couldn't tell if Orin had seen the boys or not. If he heard what Dad had said, he didn't let on. He just kept his eyes on his work and said nothing.

Sammie and Lydia watched as Dad and Orin and Allen worked. They put the pig in the wooden scalding trough filled with hot water, and rolled it around until every part was well scalded and the hair came out easily when pulled. Using the pig scrapers, they removed all the hair, hung the pig up like the beef, slit it longways down the belly with a knife, and removed the insides. At last they cut down both sides of the pig's backbone with a meat saw and left the pork to cool in the brisk winter air.

Next they quartered the beef and took it down from where it had hung all week. One by one they carried the quarters to the washhouse and put them on the long meat bench to be cut up.

Now everyone was working in the washhouse. Suddenly Sammie saw all of them looking at him and laughing. He couldn't tell what they were laughing about, so he looked at Mom.

"Look behind you," Mom said.

Sammie turned around, but he could see nothing.

"No," Mom said, "feel your pants seat."

Someone had pinned the pig's tail to his pant seat! He looked around. There was only one person in the washhouse who would do that, Orin Graber. Orin was laughing as hard as he could while pretending to pay close attention to his work.

Once the beef was finished, the pork was brought in to be cut up. Sammie waited a good while until the others were busily cutting the sides of pork into hams, bacon, canning meat and scraps for sausage, and had forgotten about Orin's practical joke. While Orin was hard at work, Sammie sneaked up behind him and pinned the tail on his pants seat!

Now everyone was laughing at Orin and he couldn't figure out why. Suddenly he reached behind and turned red in the face. All the others held their sides from laughing so hard. "I guess the last laugh is always the best one," Dad teased him.

Sammie felt pretty good about that. Orin was always teasing him, and now he had gotten one back!

In the afternoon Mom and Mrs. Graber emptied the pig's intestines and washed them thoroughly. Next they turned them inside out and scraped the inside skin off with little blocks of wood. After they washed them again, they weren't intestines any more, but sausage casings. Leaving the casings in a bowl of water, they went to season the sausage meat.

The men had ground up all the pork scraps and dumped them on the table. Mom and Mrs. Graber put salt and pepper and spices over the pile of meat and worked it in with their hands.

Dad got the sausage stuffer from the attic and set it up in the washhouse. Mom filled the stuffer with ground sausage, then took the casings from the water and slipped them all over the spout at the base of the stuffer. As Allen Graber slowly turned the handle, Mom guided the ground sausage into the casings. When the first casing was full, she found the end of the next one and started again. Allen knew just how fast to crank and Mom knew just how to handle the casings. Mrs. Graber turned the bowl underneath so the sausage could flow into the bowl without twisting. Everything worked together, and in the end there were two large bowls of smooth brown sausage coiled up like thick rope.

Finally the meat was cut up, and all that was left was a basket of fat from the pig, which was divided into little cubes ready for rendering. Dad set up a large kettle in the yard near the back door and built a fire underneath. He put the fat in and stirred it as it sizzled and steamed. Gradually the fat melted and liquid lard began to form. After a long time, Dad pulled out little pieces of skin to check them. When the skin had little white pimples on it, Dad said the rendering was finished.

Dad brought the sausage stuffer outside to use as a lard press, and ladled the rendered lard into it. As he turned the handle, the hot liquid lard flowed out of the bottom into a can. He kept pressing until no more lard came out, and all that was left in the press was a thin cake of cracklings. After it cooled, the lard would be thick and white, ready for use in Mom's baking recipes.

Dad broke off bits of cracklings and ate them. He also handed one to Sammie. They were good, so Sammie began eating bigger pieces.

"Be careful," Dad warned, "cracklings are rich and can give you a sick stomach." Sammie had already eaten enough, so he had to stop.

The meat cutting was all done and it was time for the Grabers to go home. There were still hams and bacons to cure and lots of meat chunks and sausage to can, but, because it was cold out, that all could wait until later. Only the liverwurst needed to be made before they could stop for the day, but now it was chore time, so the liverwurst was left to be done after chores were finished.

When they came to the barn, the little yellow tiger kitten was nowhere to be seen. Sammie told Dad and Mom what he had seen that forenoon.

"Those boys should have their seats warmed up. All the nonsense they get into. One of them is liable to get kicked, the way they act around horses," Dad said, and told Mom what the boys had done with Mollie and Dollie.

After milking Dad helped Sammie look for the yellow tiger kitten. They finally found it sitting on a beam.

"Here, hold the lantern," Dad said, handing it to Sammie. He climbed up and brought the kitten down.

"Nice kitty, nice kitty," he said, gently stroking it.

The kitten spat and clawed and hissed and tried to get away. But Dad held it firmly and kept stroking until it settled down. Next he set it down before a pan of milk. It drank hungrily and didn't run away when Dad petted it, but after that the little yellow tiger kitten wasn't as tame as the others.

After chores were over, Dad emptied the water out of the kettle and built the fire up again under it. During the day the women had cooked the bones of both the beef and pork and picked off all the bits of meat. The hearts and part of the livers were also cooked, then spices were added, and it was all ground up to make the liverwurst. Finally, Dad put it in the kettle and fried the fat out so that it would taste better and not be so rich.

It was late when they finished, and they were all very tired, but butchering day was finally over.

"Dad?" Lydia asked when they were sitting in the living room getting ready to go to bed.

"Yes, what do you want, Lydia?" Dad answered.

"Doesn't it hurt the pig and the steer when you butcher them?" Lydia asked.

"We kill them quickly," Dad answered, "that way they don't suffer. Today the pig was dead before it knew anything had happened. Even then, we don't just kill an animal for fun. You see, I don't want you children or Mom or Baby David to go hungry. That is why we butchered a pig and a steer. We don't kill an animal unless we have a good reason to, such as using it for food. Do you understand?"

Sammie and Lydia both nodded.

"Maybe I should tell you a story that happened when I was a little boy," Dad said then.

"Yes, yes, do!" The children said together.

They brought their little benches and Dannie sat on Dad's knee to listen to the story.

"When I was a little boy," Dad began, "some people from the city came out to the farm and wanted to buy a butcher pig. Your grandfather sold them one, and he expected them to take it alive. But then the man climbed right into the pig pen and sliced the pig's throat while it was still alive. Of course it hurt the pig and it ran around squealing until it bled to death. Then they threw a pile of straw over it and burned off the hair and took out the insides before taking it home."

"Your grandfather wasn't happy about that and none of us liked to see a pig killed that way. After that whenever anyone came to buy an animal, Grandfather always asked first how they were going to take it or how they would kill it and so forth. He didn't want an animal killed like that on his farm again."

"Did it ever happen again?" Sammie asked.

"No, it never did," Dad answered.

"I'm glad that we don't butcher our pigs that way." Lydia said.

"Me too," Sammie added, "And I'm glad that your gun doesn't have six shots in it all at once."

Now Dad laughed, "Hard telling if that ever really happened. But it does make a funny story."

"Anyway, children," Dad went on, "It isn't just killing that is cruel. You must always remember to be nice to animals. Never torment an animal for fun. That is not a good thing to do. Do you understand?"

All three of the children nodded. Sammie sat thinking. Poking a kitten with a fork or throwing it in a water tank was cruel, too. He understood what Dad meant.

After a few days the meat was all processed, but Mom's work didn't let up. In less than two weeks, church services would be held in their home. That was how it worked. Every family in the church took their turn about once every eight months or so. The last services had been at Orin Grabers, and the church benches, hymn books and dishes for the noon meal were there, so Dad had to take the wagon over to Graber's and bring them home. When the time came for Church Sunday, the benches would be set up in the living room and kitchen for the services.

Mom fussed and worked hard to get everything cleaned and straightened up. There were windows to clean, floors and walls to scrub, furniture to dust, curtains to wash and iron, stoves to black, plus food to be prepared. While she was doing this, all the other work of the home still had to go on. Mom was very busy.

"Maybe you should do like my dad used to say," Dad told Mom one day.

"How was that? Mom asked.

"My dad used to say that all you needed to do to get ready for church was pour out the slop bucket and hang up a clean hand towel," Dad laughed.

"Well, that may be, but when would we ever clean if we didn't do it to have church in our home?" Mom said.

"I guess we can be happy that we have it in the dead of winter. There is snow on the ground, so we don't have to cut grass or clean up much outside," Dad said.

"Yes, I'm glad about that, too" Mom said, nodding. She went back to her cleaning as before.

Chapter 10

Church Sunday

"Run upstairs and bring me a jar of apple schnitz," Mom told Sammie one day.

Sammie knew where they were. He remembered the day in early fall when Aunt Lena and Mrs. Graber had been there to help Mom peel apples and slice them into little pieces. Then Sammie had helped her fill the trays of the little drying house next to the woodshed. When it was full, she had built a little fire under it to slowly dehydrate the apple pieces. After the slices had dried, they were put into gallon jars and set in the spare room upstairs. The children liked to eat the rubbery apple schnitz, but today Mom wanted to use them to bake half-moon pies.

Mom took the jar from Sammie and put the right amount of schnitz in a large pan. She added a little water and some sugar and spice, and set the pan on the stove to cook. With a long wooden spoon, she stirred the schnitz so it wouldn't set up in the bottom of the pan and scorch, which would give the schnitz a burned flavor. It was very important that this batch of half-moon pies turn out right, because Mom was baking them for church.

When the schnitz was well cooked, Mom took it from the stove and put the mixture through a ricer, making a bowl of smooth, brown schnitz pie filling.

While the mixture was cooking, Mom had put together a batch of pie dough. Now she took a small handful of it and squeezed it, passing it back and forth from one hand to the other until it was round and smooth. Next she took the rolling pin from the drawer and covered it with a thin layer of flour. She also sprinkled some flour on the counter before she put down the dough, and then some flour on top of the ball of dough so that the dough wouldn't stick to anything when she rolled it out.

When the dough had been rolled thin enough, Mom put a large spoonful of filling in the middle. She then carefully picked up the one side of the dough and folded it over, making what looked like a half-moon. With her fingers, she crimped a half circle where the edge of the pie was going to be and, with a knife, cut off the extra dough along the curved edge. These little pies were finally placed on a cookie sheet and put into the toasty, hot oven. After a while, Mom took out bubbling, hot, half-moon pies.

Mom's hands fairly flew when she baked. Sammie loved to watch. He wondered how she could move so fast without doing the wrong things. But, in the end, there were delicious, golden brown half-moon pies. They were just the right color, just the right size, and just the right shape. And they were very good to eat!

But Sammie and Lydia and Dannie weren't allowed to eat any now. All the little pies had to be kept for the small children to eat in church, which in only three more days would be at their house.

Those three days were filled with work. Aunt Lena, Mrs. Graber and Mrs. Mullet came to help. They washed the windows inside and out. Aunt Lena mopped the porch floor and Mrs. Graber cleaned the washhouse. Mrs. Mullet cleaned and blackened the stoves. All of them helped Mom move furniture out of the way to make room for the church benches. Sammie helped with this, too. All the while Mom was putting up clean window curtains and restoring clean throw carpets to their places throughout the house.

By Saturday all was clean, and it was time to get the food ready. Until church was over, the children weren't allowed to play with toys which made a mess. Sammie and Lydia went to the root cellar and brought back jar after jar of pickled red beets and pickled cucumbers and apple butter and blackberry jelly. They weren't allowed to walk into the clean kitchen with their snowy boots, either, so they set the jars inside the washhouse door. When they were done bringing food from the root cellar, they took off their boots and carried the jars from the washhouse into the kitchen.

Of course Dad had a lot of work, too. He cleaned the whole barn and hauled load after load of manure out and spread it on the fields. After that he took the straw hook and pulled straw from the stack behind the barn. It took a bunch of straw to bed the whole barn, and that was a job Sammie could help with. Dad carried it in by the forkful and Sammie spread it out nicely in the stalls. In the end the whole barn wore a clean look. Every stall had a new bed of silky yellow oat straw.

Even the calf pen was clean and had new bedding. The calves sniffed at the new straw and frisked about to show their pleasure.

* * * * * *

In the afternoon Dad hitched Mollie and Dollie to the wagon and drove over to the Grabers to get the church benches. He and Orin loaded the benches on the wagon, and Dad brought them home. Just before supper, he set them up in the living room and kitchen. Now everything was ready except the last minute things.

For supper, Mom set out sandwiches and milk. The house looked strange and it seemed odd to eat sitting on the benches. But the table was full of food to be used the next day and Mom didn't want to dirty up a lot of dishes. After supper the children took their baths, and went off to bed.

Sammie lay in his bed thinking. Tomorrow church would actually be at their house. He could hardly believe it! It had been almost a whole year since they last hosted church, and he could barely remember.

He could hear Dad and Mom still moving around downstairs and he thought he was going to stay awake a long time. But suddenly he awoke and heard Mom calling him for chores.

It was morning, and they had to hurry! The chores were done earlier than usual and breakfast was eaten quickly. Mom hurried through the house doing last minute "this 'n that's" and Dad helped Dannie into his Sunday clothes. Already Mom had put on her dark blue broadcloth dress with a white starched cape and apron neatly pinned over it, and her head covering was tied with a small bow under her chin.

Finally everything seemed ready, but Mom was still working. Buggies came down the highway and turned in at the driveway. They each stopped by the washhouse door and the women and girls stepped down and quickly went in out of the cold.

Sammie ran out to watch. The men drove their rigs to the barn and unhitched. Dad's cattle and horses were in the barnyard so there was room in the barn for all the horses that came.

Uncle Andy came driving up with his team. His horses never liked to stand. Steam rose from their sweaty coats and they tossed their heads and pranced impatiently. But Uncle Andy held firmly to the lines and made them stop. Aunt Lena and the girls got down and quickly stepped away from the wheels. Just as soon as he could, Uncle

Andy loosened the reins and the horses went away toward the barn to be unhitched.

When all the people were there, they began filing into the house. The women and girls filled up one side of the living room and part of the kitchen. The men and boys sat on the other side of the living room. The ministers came in first, then the older men, and so on until all were seated. Dad and Sammie came in last because they were the hosts.

With everyone seated, the house seemed very full. But even with all the people in there, it was quiet except for the occasional cry from a baby or the creak of a bench.

At 9 A.M. the bishop announced that it was time to begin services. Another man loudly said the page number of the first song so all could hear. A song leader began singing and the rest joined in. At the end of the first line, the ministers got to their feet and went upstairs to their council room.

All the voices blended together singing a slow tune of a hymn from the thick black hymn book. Sammie loved the sound. When he was younger, he sometimes stopped his ears with his fingers, quickly opening and closing them to produce a wa-wa-wa-wow sound. He was tempted again, but Dad had often told him, "You are old enough to sit still and behave."

So he tried to sit still. But after a while his legs grew tired from dangling and his back ached. He thought of laying his head on Dad's lap and resting a bit. But he couldn't do that now. Dad was holding Dannie. He squirmed and tried to find a more comfortable position. Dad glanced his way, so he tried to sit still.

He looked around at the other people. The big girls sat prim and straight on the first bench of the women's side. Every girl shared a hymn book with the next person and paid strict attention to the singing.

One woman was having trouble with her toddling little boy. He refused to sit still and cried out loud. She tried to keep him content with a toy, but he threw it down and cried some more. Now the woman got to her feet and picked up the boy. Sammie saw her go through the washhouse door, and he knew exactly what was going to happen.

Little children were allowed to eat or play with toys in church, but they must learn to be quiet and not cause a disturbance. When that happened, their father or mother took them outside and spanked them.

Mom's rocking chair was in the bedroom and Sammie watched as a woman with a tiny baby got up and went in there. The chair was there on purpose so mothers would have a place to feed their babies and rock them to sleep.

The woman with the toddler returned and sat down. The little boy was still weeping silently, but he made no more loud noises. Soon he laid his head on his mother's lap and went to sleep.

The ministers returned while the congregation was still singing. Very soon the song stopped and the first minister got up to preach the opening sermon. After a while they all knelt to pray, and then stood while another minister read from the Bible. When he finished, they all sat down and yet another minister got up to preach the main sermon.

Then came the part Sammie had been looking forward to. Mom had a large bowl of half-moon pies and was passing them out to children. Sammie was glad it wasn't next year, because then he'd be going to school, and he'd be too old to eat in church. The pies were so the little children wouldn't get so hungry. On church Sunday, breakfast was early and dinner was late.

Sammie sat and enjoyed his half-moon pie. He looked around the room. Cousin Jonas sat next to his Dad without a pie. He was in first grade, so he was too old to eat in church.

After the main sermon, they knelt while the minister led in prayer. Then came the closing song and the church service was over. It had lasted three hours.

All the boys quickly got up and went out for some fresh air. The men walked outside or stood around visiting.

In the living room and the kitchen where the people had sat for the services, the benches were pushed together to make tables. The women scurried around and quickly filled them with bread and butter and apple butter and blackberry jelly and pickled red beets and cucumbers.

In a short time Dad called everyone in to eat. They all sat on benches and ate from the long tables which had been formed from benches, and which were the same height as the benches they sat on.

After dinner the boys went outside to play. Some of the ladies washed the dishes and put them away. Throughout the house men, women, and girls visited. Little children played on the floor and babies fussed.

Starting at about 2:30 P.M., families began hitching up their horses to their buggies and leaving. The sun sank lower and lower in the western sky, and finally everybody had gone home.

It was sundown when Dad and Sammie headed for the barn to do chores. They had to hurry. The young folks of the church would be coming back for supper and hymn singing.

Sammie had really looked forward to that, but he was tired. He sat and slowly ate his supper. Mom had made escalloped potatoes with bits of pork in it and baked beans and apple sauce. For dessert she served mixed fruit and cake. It was a very good supper.

Then the young folks began singing and Dad and Sammie went to the living room. Sammie loved to hear them sing, but he grew tired. Finally he laid his head on Dad's lap. The singing gradually drifted farther and farther away until it was gone, and Sammie was fast asleep.

The next day Dad and Mom and the children were busy putting things back in order and piling the church benches on the front porch. This was something Sammie and Lydia could help with. With one of them on each end, they carried bench after bench onto the porch until they were all out of the house.

There was plenty of food left over, so Mom didn't cook any dinner. They didn't sit at the table either.

"Go wash your hands, then you can eat your dinner," Mom told them. "My hands aren't dirty," Sammie said, holding them up for her to see. But Mom would hear no such thing! "You go wash your hands!" she insisted. So he did. He was surprised at how much dirt was in the water when he finished, so he quickly poured the water down the drain so no one else would see.

"Find a place to sit so you don't spill your food," Mom said then.

The food was good even if it was leftovers, and, at the end, each child was allowed to have a half-moon pie. That was the best of all. Sammie could eat half-moon pies every day of the year if he had them.

By evening the house was back in order. Church at their house was over. In two weeks it would move on to the next place, and so on. It would be a long time before their turn would come again. That was the way it was. Every other Sunday was church Sunday and the in between Sunday was for visiting and resting.

Chapter 11

The New Coloring Book

In the middle of January the weather warmed up. Dad said it was a regular January thaw. The snow melted and the ice on the driveway became thinner.

"It feels like spring," Dad said one morning, "I'm almost itching to get the plow out."

"Well, you can't expect the warm weather to last at this time of the year," Mom said.

"It's good though while it's here," Dad answered, "A person can work outside without bundling up so thick."

"Well, I'd rather have snow," Mom said, "No matter how hard we try, the mud from the outside always finds it's way onto the floors."

Dad looked at the children. He looked down at their shoes and said, "You know what overshoes are for." That was all, but it meant that they must not go out again without overshoes.

That very night it turned colder and snowed, and Mom got her wish. There was no more mud. The world was clean and fresh and white. The snow had come down softly without a wind, and every branch, post, and roof was loaded with it.

"Isn't it ever pretty!" Mom said that morning when Dad and Sammie came in for breakfast after chores.

Dad set down the two buckets of coal he had brought in, took off his gloves, and held his hands over the stove to warm them.

"Yes, you sure can't beat it for looks," Dad said laughing. "But looks isn't everything."

"Are you just talking about the weather?" Mom asked smiling.

And Sammie knew that Dad and Mom were teasing each other. He knew that Dad didn't mind the snow, because it kept the strawberries and the hay from being frozen out, and it kept the water pipes underground from freezing shut. And Mom didn't mind warm spring-like days. But mud on the floors was work to clean, so they couldn't blame her for not appreciating that.

It was time to sell the calves which had been sick last fall. Dad needed to use a telephone to call for a truck to take them away, so that forenoon he went over to the Gressingers.

"Let's hurry and see if we can have dinner ready when Dad comes back," Mom told the children after he left. "Lydia, you may set the table, and Sammie, you may run to the root cellar and bring a jar of applesauce and a jar of peaches."

Then she set to work. She had some green beans and chicken left over from the day before. She quickly toasted some bread crumbs, and put them into a large skillet, together with the leftovers. Next she added in some butter and poured in enough milk to moisten everything. As it heated, Mom kept stirring the mixture so it wouldn't stick to the bottom and scorch. Finally it was bubbling hot, and she put in some salt and spices. She tasted it, closed her eyes while thinking what else was needed, then added a little more salt and a few more spices and tasted it again. It was now ready, and she pushed the skillet back to where the stove wasn't as hot.

No matter what leftovers Mom started out with, she always ended up with a delicious, filling meal. Dad called those mixtures hash, but he liked them, too.

Now dinner was ready, but Dad wasn't home yet. They waited a while, but he didn't come. Baby David was fussy and Dannie was tired and ready for his afternoon nap.

"Let's sit down and eat, children," Mom finally said, "I can keep some food warm for Dad, and he can eat when he comes. I wonder what's keeping him so long?"

So they sat down to the table and ate Mom's good hash and applesauce and homemade bread with apple butter on it.

When they were finished with that, they each took some peaches for dessert. Just then they heard Dad come into the washhouse and stamp the snow from his boots. He came in and took his seat at the table before saying anything.

"Whatever kept you so long?" Mom asked then.

"Oh, just talking," Dad answered. He dished out the food on his plate and went on, "The Gressingers are going to move. Mr. Gressinger and I suddenly found a whole bunch of things to visit about. I sure hate to see them go."

"Yes, I hate to lose such good neighbors," Mom returned.

"Of course, I suppose if we are good neighbors, we will have good neighbors, no matter who lives there." Dad said, "That holds true at least ninety percent of the time."

"Yes, of course," Mom said, "But we are so used to the Gressingers, and they are always so friendly and kind. It's hard to see them go."

In the afternoon Mom sent Sammie to the root cellar to get a jar of blackberry jelly. She put it in a brown paper bag along with some freshly baked cookies and a loaf of bread.

"Sammie and Lydia, you may take this to the Gressingers," Mom said. "Watch out so you don't break this jar and don't squeeze too much because there is a loaf of bread in here. Be careful when you cross the road. Look both ways and make sure there are no cars coming before you go across."

The Gressingers lived back from the road. They had a nice home with trees in the yard and a freshly painted red barn farther back.

Mrs. Gressinger opened the door when Sammie knocked.

"Hi, children," she greeted them, "Come on in. Is there something I can do for you?"

They stepped inside and Sammie handed the bag to her.

"Oh, thank you!" she exclaimed, looking into the bag.

She gave them chairs to sit on and asked them lots of questions, but the children just looked at her shyly and said nothing. If they knew the answer to the question, they nodded or shook their head.

But Mrs. Gressinger was very friendly, and gradually they forgot their shyness. She kept on talking, and Sammie began to answer back out loud. If he didn't know the answer in English, he said it in German. She kept on visiting and didn't seem to mind.

Sammie looked around the kitchen. It was different than Mom's. The Gressingers were young and didn't have any children. There was a small table standing in the middle of the kitchen. It had a beautiful checkered cloth over it and two blue placemats on spots in front of the two chairs.

Sammie's eyes went on over to the refrigerator. There was a flowered hand towel hanging from it's door handle. Next to the refrigerator on the counter top was a shiny black toaster. The walls were papered with a flower pattern and the ceiling was yellow. The whole kitchen looked clean and fresh.

"Here," Mrs. Gressinger said.

Sammie looked back at her.

"How about some suckers," she said holding them out to the children.

They each took one and Sammie said, "Thank you."

He pushed Lydia and she said, "Thank you."

Then she gave them another sucker for Dannie, and they went home. They could hardly believe their good fortune! What a treat!

The next day Mrs. Gressinger came over to visit with Mom. She was sorry to be leaving their home in the country, but Mr. Gressinger had a new job, so it would be better for them to move to the city.

Before she left, she handed a brown paper bag to Lydia and said to Mom, "Here is a little something for the children."

"What do you say, children?" Mom asked.

Sammie and Lydia immediately thanked her and Dannie said "Thank you" after Mom helped him.

"You're welcome," Mrs. Gressinger said, "I hope you will enjoy it." Then she went out the door and headed home.

The children couldn't wait to see what was in there. Sammie and Dannie crowded close as Lydia took out a beautiful coloring book and a box of brand new colors.

Sammie tried to get a hold of it, but Lydia pulled it back.

"She gave it to me," she said.

"Now, now, Lydia," Mom chided, "She said it was for you all. Here, why don't you sit down together and look at it."

She helped them as Sammie and Lydia sat on their little benches with Dannie between them.

"There, that looks better," Mom said, "Why don't we put the colors away until Sunday? That way you'll have something new again."

She put the colors in the cabinet.

The children didn't look very far until Sammie knew which picture he wanted to color first. On one page was a picture of a beautiful colt.

"Mom, may I have the colors right away?" he asked.

"No, Sammie, wait until Sunday. You can look at the pictures today, and we'll get out the colors on Sunday. That way the treat will last longer.

That Sunday was in-between Sunday, which meant that there would be no church services. Outside the weather was snowy and cold, and Dad and Mom were glad to stay inside the warm house and rest.

As soon as the breakfast dishes were done, Mom let the children have the new box of colors.

Lydia picked them up and said, "I'm going to color first."

But Sammie had the coloring book and he wouldn't give it to her. They stood there glaring at each other until Mom said, "Let Sammie color first. He is older."

Lydia slowly laid the colors on the table. She had to do what Mom said, but she didn't stop glaring.

"It's not fair!" she said quietly enough so Dad and Mom wouldn't hear.

But Sammie thought it was fair. After all he couldn't help that he was the oldest. Besides, he would be starting school next year, and it was important that he learn to color well. He found the picture of the colt and colored it.

Then it was Lydia's turn. She found a picture of a little circus dog balancing a ball on his nose.

"It isn't as nice as mine," Sammie told her.

She made a face at him and quick as a flash she slapped him.

Sammie tried to duck, but he was too late. She hit him square in the face, and it hurt. He pulled back his hand and hit Lydia back as hard as he could.

"Ouch!" Lydia wailed.

Dad and Mom were both sitting in the living room reading, but Dad could see them through the doorway.

"Sammie!" Dad said sharply, "Come here."

Sammie wished he didn't have to go, but there was no way out. He walked toward Dad with his head down.

"She hit me first," Sammie said.

"Lydia, you may come, too," Dad said then.

"He said his picture was nicer than mine," Lydia said.

"You must never hit each other. Surely you knew better, didn't you?" Dad asked.

They both nodded.

"Even if someone else hits you first, you must not," Dad said. "The Bible tells us that if someone hits us on the right cheek, we should turn the other also. And, Sammie, you surely know better than to brag on your own picture, don't you?"

Sammie nodded.

Dad spanked them both and made them sit on their little benches to get over their crossness.

Sammie sat thinking. Why did he always get in trouble? Why was it so hard to be good? He had thought Lydia was worse because she had hit him first. But Dad had punished them the same. Some things were hard to understand.

Dad was reading again, while Mom sat slowly rocking Baby David and softly singing:

Wo ist Jesus, mein verlangen,	*Where is Jesus, whom I long for,*
Mein geliebter, Herr und Freund;	*My beloved, Lord and friend;*
Wo ist er den hingegangen,	*Where had He then gone to,*
Wo mag er zu finden sein.	*Where is He to be found.*

Sammie went on thinking. Everything was peaceful in the house and Dannie had the coloring book and was happily scribbling away. Sammie wished he could help Dannie do a better job, but he had to stay seated until Dad said he could go. He looked at Lydia. At least she had to sit, too.

Mom took Baby David to the bedroom and laid him in his crib. When she came back, she picked up Dannie from the floor and sat back on her chair. Then she said, "Now, children, pull your benches over here and I'll tell you a story."

Dad looked up from his reading and nodded to them, so they knew it was okay to move.

Mom told them the story of Joseph and his brothers. That was one of Sammie's favorite Bible stories. As he sat there listening, his anger toward Lydia went gradually away. The story, and the way Mom told it, softened his little heart until he was sure he didn't want to be bad like Joseph's brothers. He would be nice to Lydia and Dannie and Baby David and be like Joseph.

That afternoon Sammie and Lydia put on their wraps and went out to play in the snow. All afternoon they played nicely and didn't quarrel at all.

In the days that followed, the weather remained cold. Work on the little farm slacked off. Church at their house was past, and butchering was finished. The calves in the lean-to were sold, and that made fewer chores. Dad and Mom weren't as busy, so the evening chores were done earlier. That meant there would be longer evenings by the stove before bedtime. The time of the year had come again for homemade ice cream and cozy times around the living room heater.

Chapter 12

Winter Pleasures

After the Gressingers moved, Harold Neare and his wife came to live on the farm across the road. They were an elderly couple and very friendly.

One day soon after they moved in, Harold came to visit with Dad. Sammie couldn't wait to get a good look at him, because Dad had said that he was a detective. That meant that he had the job of finding and catching bad people or figuring out who had done bad things. Dad had explained all this to the children.

Sammie looked him up and down. He wore a small gray felt hat like most of the other neighbors did when they dressed up and a long coat, which was buckled around his middle. He didn't look much different than other people, but there was an air of excitement about him. From what Dad said, being a detective must be very exciting and important work.

"Sammie," Mom said from the kitchen, motioning for Sammie to come. "You must not stare at people. That is bad manners."

So Sammie sat on his little bench in the living room and listened to the men talk. Once in a while he took a good look at Harold. But he remembered what Mom said and, in a moment, looked away again.

"I think we'll have good neighbors again," Dad said after Harold had gone home. "I suppose it is just like I said before. If we treat our neighbors right, we'll have good neighbors."

"Yes, I suppose," Mom agreed.

Then Dad went whistling out the door to his work. He had to shovel snow so the milk man could come in the driveway to pick up their milk.

The windows in the house were frozen shut, and there were many kinds of pretty designs all over them. Some looked like stars, some were shaped like leaves, and some looked like waves in water.

Sammie and Lydia and Dannie breathed against the window panes and quickly wiped the moisture off with their handkerchiefs. Through the clear opening they could watch Dad at his work. In a minute the window froze over again and the vision blurred, but they could still see Dad's dark form move back and forth as he shoveled snow.

When the weather was cold, it took a lot of corn cobs and firewood to keep the stoves going. Every day the two woodboxes had to be filled, and every day cobs had to be brought in for the kitchen range. Sammie and Lydia got very tired of filling them.

But at night everything was comfortable and warm in the house. Dad would sit in his rocking chair reading *THE BUDGET* or one of his farm magazines. Mom would sit in her rocker holding Baby David in one arm and reading the new almanac which she held in the other. Dannie played with toys on the floor, and Sammie and Lydia sat on their little benches with their feet on the bottom flange of the round living room heater. They were sharing the big blue Bible story book and looking at the pictures.

"Dad," Sammie said.

"Yes, Sammie, what do you want?" asked Dad as he looked up from his reading.

"Dad, did you have to carry wood when you were small?" Sammie asked.

"I sure did. And it was worse for me, because all my brothers and sisters were bigger, and I had to do it alone. You two should be glad that you can share the work," Dad said.

"But is takes so long to get done," Sammie said then.

"Maybe I should tell you the story of the day when it got dark when I was a boy," Dad said laying his paper aside.

"Yes, do," the children chimed together. They moved their benches close to Dad's chair and Dannie climbed on his lap.

"When I was about your age," Dad said looking at Sammie, "I had to carry all the wood for the stoves in our house. And of course, like you, I got tired of it."

"One day my father and big brothers were cutting logs in the woods, but I had to stay home to help my mother around the house. She told me to bring in wood so she could cook a good dinner. Father and my brothers would naturally be hungry when they came in at noon."

"Well," Dad went on, "right across the road from our house some men had set up a sawmill. It was powered by a great big steam engine and it was all quite a sight for me. On my way to get wood, I stopped to watch the sawing. I meant to go right on with wood carrying, but I got so absorbed in watching that I forgot about the wood."

"The fireman kept building the fire in the boiler and the engine kept hissing and steaming and chugging, and the pulleys and belts kept spinning as the men sawed log after log. Smoke rose from the big stack at the front end of the boiler until the air was thick with it. The smoke seemed to hide the sun and suddenly, the day got darker and darker.

I ran in and told my mother to come out and see what a big smoke the steam engine was making. "

"When Mother came out, she told me that the darkness wasn't caused by the smoke as I thought. Something else was the cause, but she didn't know what. Here it was in the middle of the day and it was almost totally dark."

"What made it dark?" Sammie asked leaning forward on his little bench.

"I thought maybe it was the end of the world," Dad went on, "And I remembered suddenly that I should have carried my wood. I felt very naughty and quickly ran to fill the woodbox."

"Was it the end of the world?" Lydia asked, wide-eyed.

"No, of course not," Dad answered, "And after a short time the light came back. But when my father and brothers came in, dinner wasn't ready and it was all my fault. Mother didn't have the right kind of wood, so the dinner cooked slowly and wasn't done."

"My father then told us that there had been an eclipse of the sun, and that was what made it dark. But I remembered the lesson a long time. You should always do your things the way you would want to be doing them when the end of the world comes."

Sammie and Lydia sat on their little benches and thought. Then Sammie asked, "Dad, what is an eclipse?"

"It is when the moon passes in front of the sun. Sometimes it only covers a little of it and you hardly notice. But when it shuts off the sun's light then it gets dark even if it is in the middle of the day." Dad explained.

That was the end of the story and it was bed time.

It was still cold when the first of February came, but the sun shone warmer. The snow on the roofs melted and water dripped off the edge to be refrozen by the cold air into long icicles. These icicles hung so low from the washhouse roof that the children could reach them. When they were outside playing or carrying wood, they broke off pieces and sucked them like popsicles.

The next day was Ground Hog Day. It was a sunny day, and at dinner time Dad said the ground hog was sure to see its shadow.

"Why, Dad?' Sammie asked.

"Oh, there is an old saying," Dad explained, "that on February second the ground hog comes out of her hole in the ground after sleeping all winter. If she doesn't see her shadow, she stays out and spring will soon be here."

"What happens when she sees her shadow?" Sammie asked.

"Well, then they say she is scared back in and sleeps another six weeks, and that spring won't come until she wakes up again," Dad said smiling a little.

Sammie wondered how a ground hog could possibly control the coming of spring. The only groundhog he had ever seen was the one Sport killed and brought up to the buildings.

"I suppose if the ground hog sees her shadow, we're bound to have another six weeks of winter," Dad said laughing. "If she doesn't see her shadow, it will only be a month and a half!"

Sammie couldn't quite figure it out.

"Six weeks and a month and a half are the same thing," Mom explained.

Now it made sense to Sammie. Dad didn't believe that the ground hog had anything to do with it. Spring would come approximately six weeks or a month and a half after February second. Sometimes a little earlier and sometimes a little later regardless what the ground hog did.

That evening the family was going to make home-made ice cream with the Eli Mullets, who were coming to visit.

After chores were finished, Dad took his ax and knocked down the icicles that hung from the washhouse roof. With Sammie's help, Dad picked up the ice and put it in a burlap feed sack. Dad laid the sack of ice on the concrete slab just outside the door, and, with the flat side of his ax, pounded until the ice was well crushed. He then poured the crushed ice into a bucket, and they were ready to begin freezing ice cream.

Mom had put the proper ingredients together earlier and set the can out to cool. Dad set the can inside the freezer and fastened the crank.

"Do you want to turn, Sammie?" Dad asked.

Sammie took the handle and began turning. It went easy to begin with. Dad poured some crushed ice into the freezer around the can and added a little salt. Then he took a stick and punched it down all around the can, mixing the salt well into the ice.

The crank turned a bit harder and Sammie began getting tired. He stopped to rest for a moment, but Dad said "Don't stop turning, Sammie." And Sammie knew why he said that. If you stopped turning while the ice cream was freezing, the dasher inside the can would stick fast and would then be hard to get started again.

While Sammie was cranking, the Mullets arrived and Eli took the handle from Sammie. Mrs. Mullet stuck her head out the door and said to Eli, "Are you sure you have salt?" She laughed and went back in.

Eli told them why she was teasing him. "Once when we were first married, I wanted to make ice cream. I went into the kitchen and got what I thought was a bag of white salt. Well, I kept turning the handle for a long time and nothing happened. The cream didn't freeze at all. Finally my wife came out and discovered that I was using white sugar by mistake!"

"She doesn't let you forget that, does she?" Dad laughed.

Dad took the handle and turned. Sammie didn't understand how it worked. There was something about salt that made ice melt faster and become much colder, and help the cream inside the can get colder and freeze. Finally, it turned so hard that even Dad got tired.

He stopped and said "Let's see what we have."

He opened the can and inside was smoothly frozen ice cream. The top was swirled beautifully where the dasher had gone around.

"Yep, it's done," Dad said with a satisfied look. He pulled the can out of the ice and carried it into the kitchen.

Mom had supper ready. For dessert they had the ice cream, and it was very good!

After supper, Sammie and Oley made shadow animals. They sat on chairs between the light and the wall. With their hands they made shadows on the wall that looked like the head of a dog or a cat or a wolf or a pig. They imitated the sounds of those animals and it was great fun.

All too soon it was time for the Mullets to go home, because it was already past bedtime. Before they left, however, Sammie and Oley played tag. The game was to see who could be the last to touch the other when they parted. They kept going back and forth until Oley managed to tag Sammie and slip out the door before Sammie could tag him back. Sammie had to give up and admit that he had lost that time.

On other winter evenings, the children played games. Sometimes Mom helped them play "I Spy" or "Hide and Seek." Dannie didn't understand those games very well, and Sammie thought he spoiled the fun. But Mom didn't think so. "Let him help," she said. "That's how he learns. You didn't know how the first time you tried either."

When they were tired of playing, they would again beg for a story. Dad and Mom told them many different stories, but there were a few which were favorites. The children asked for those over and over.

One story Dad told was about when he went to school. The teacher had told the pupils about gravity, and about how it was a force that kept people from falling away from the earth. After the speech, the teacher dismissed the class, but one little boy stayed in his seat.

The teacher asked, "Johnny, why don't you leave?"

"Because," the little boy answered, "gravity is holding me down to the earth!"

Dad always laughed when he told that story. Sammie thought it was funny, too, but he didn't understand how gravity worked. As far as he could see things just stayed on the earth, and they just did, and just did!

Then the children would beg Dad to tell the "Sim Kurtz" story.

"Please! Please!" they said. And if they begged hard enough, he'd tell it.

THE SIM KURTZ STORY

"Many years ago a man by the name of Sim Kurtz lived in the hills of Holmes County, Ohio. In those days there were all kinds of wild animals in the woods such as bears, panthers, wildcats, wolves, deer, and turkeys. Sim was a great hunter and he loved to go on long hunts to bring home fresh meat.

One fine fall day he set out on a hunt. He walked and walked but didn't find any meat to take home. When night fell, he was still far from home. He walked on through the night, but it was hard to find his way in the dark, so he finally stopped.

He was going to rest for only a moment, but he was very tired. He laid his head on some leaves at the base of a large tree and soon was fast asleep.

When Sim awoke, it was morning, but he couldn't see out. Something had covered him with leaves. He slowly sat up and peeked out. Nothing was in sight. He climbed out and shook the leaves from his clothes. He looked at the pile of leaves and thought a little. In a minute he had a plan.

He looked around and found a rotten log about the size of his own body. He placed it where he had lain and heaped leaves over it to make it appear as it had before he got up. Then he climbed a tree and waited.

Soon a mama wildcat came walking stealthily into the clearing followed by two half-grown cubs. The mama cat circled the pile of leaves and nervously swung her long tail from side to side. Next she positioned the cubs one on each side of the pile. Sim watched as the wildcat went around to the end where his head had been. Then she sprang and pounced right in on the rotten log.

But at that very minute, Sim aimed his gun and fired. The wildcat fell dead into the pile of leaves, and the cubs ran away into the woods.

Sim got down off that tree a thankful man. He knew he had had a very close call. Of course he had no trouble finding his way now, because it was daylight, and he was soon home."

* * * * * *

When the story ended, Mom said it was bedtime, but the children were too interested in talking about Sim Kurtz to want to go right away.

"I'm glad that Sim woke up before that wildcat and her cubs came back," Sammie said.

"Me, too," said Lydia.

"But I'm glad he didn't shoot the cubs," Sammie said.

"He probably couldn't have if he had wanted to. In those days they hunted with muzzle loaders and it took a few minutes to reload those guns," Dad explained.

"Come on, children," Mom urged, "time to hike to bed."

But all Sammie could think was wildcats and deep woods and things like that. The children looked at each other but didn't move.

"Go on to bed," Dad said. "Early to bed and early to rise, makes a man healthy, wealthy and wise."

Now they had to go. As they started up the stairs, Sammie made a little sound to imitate a wildcat. He wanted to scare Lydia just a little bit, but the sound came out much more fiercely than he had planned. It scared Lydia a whole lot and he even scared himself. They both took off down the stairs as fast as they could.

"Now what is wrong?" Mom asked.

"Sammie scared me," Lydia answered.

"Sammie!" Dad scolded. That was all Dad said, but it meant that he should not have done what he did.

"I didn't mean to scare her that much," Sammie said sheepishly.

Mom stood at the base of the stairs until Sammie and Lydia were in their rooms. After their prayers, they settled into their beds.

Sammie pulled the covers completely over him and shivered with fear. All he could see when he closed his eyes were wildcats and deep woods and things like that. But this didn't last long. Sammie was very tired and in no time was fast asleep.

Chapter 13

Springtime

The days were not as cold now. The mornings were still frosty, but the warm afternoon sun was gradually melting all the snow and ice. Icicles dropped from the roof edges and wasted away to nothing. Water ran into ditches, and from there to the creek, and finally into the Salamonie River. The Salamonie became swollen and overflowed its banks, and all that muddy water went churning away toward the northwest to places Sammie knew nothing about.

The ground stayed muddy until the sun dried it out. Robins came back from the sunny south and were hopping around the lawn looking for food. Overhead the Canadian geese were flying to their summer nesting places. The "honkers," as Mom called them, flew in a perfect "V" formation. They honked an irregular tune, and Sammie watched as they disappeared over the woods to the north.

Dad said spring had come for sure. The long evenings by the living room heater had come to an end, and there would be no more home-made ice cream until next winter. Dad was again putting in long days on the farm and Mom was busy in the house.

Each day the sun shone warmer. Millions of tiny green blades pushed their way up through the dead brown grasses which were matted to the ground. The oak tree in the yard and the bushes in the fence row put out multitudes of little buds, and stood holding them as if waiting for the right time to let the leaves grow out. Dad's barley field had come through the winter in good shape. The young barley plants were already growing nicely in the spring sunshine, and Dad said it was time to "seed in" (or "*ein sähen*") the barley with hay.

Dad did the seeding in the early morning before chores or breakfast. He said it had to be done when the air was still.

"That wind is bound to pick up again by mid-morning," he said.

One frosty, windless morning, Dad was already in the field by the time Sammie woke up. He had the broadcast seeder strapped to his shoulder and was spreading the seed. The seeder looked like a regular cloth flour sack with a carrying strap of strong cotton webbing, to which a flow gauge and spreading tube were fastened on the bottom.

Dad walked back and forth across the beautiful green barley field. With one hand he made sure the seed was "feeding through" properly. With the other he steadily swung the tube from side to side. Across the field he went again and again, evenly spreading the hay seed. He knew just how fast to walk and swung the tube in time with his stride. When he reached the top of the field, he knew just how far to walk across before starting back downfield again so that the whole field would be covered with hay seed.

The little hay seeds would sprout and take root while the barley grew. All summer the plants would stay small and spindly until the barley was cut. Then the hay would grow up out of the stubble, and by next summer it would be a field of good thick hay.

That day Dad began plowing. The field northeast of the barn had been in hay the year before. All winter Dad had been hauling manure and spreading it over the ground, because this year that field was to be planted in corn.

Day after day Dad walked behind the plow. Mollie and Dollie and Tim leaned into their collars and pulled with all their might. Dad drove with the driving reins around his back because it took both hands to control the plow. The plow bit into the earth and turned over furrow after furrow of smooth, fresh-looking sod. But, at one furrow at a time, it took a long time to plow the whole field.

Dad had to keep his hands on the plow handles and sometimes, when it was windy, a sudden strong gust of wind would take off his hat. It would bounce and spin over the newly plowed earth until it found a low spot and came to rest. Dad had to stop the horses and run after the hat. Then just before he reached it, the wind picked it up and the chase was on again.

"I need strings like you have," he said to Sammie once after he came back with his hat.

Mom always sewed strings on Sammie's hat. The wind could bend the brim up and down, but it had to stay on his head.

"This is something else!" Dad exclaimed at dinnertime, "I can hardly get anything done except chasing my hat! It sure makes a guy wish for hills. It is no wonder the wind blows here. The land is "flat as a pancake" and there is nothing to stop it."

Mom just smiled a little and said nothing. She understood the prairie, but Dad had grown up in the hills of Ohio and it was hard for him to get used to the winds that swept across the plains.

When Sammie got tired of following Dad in the field, he played with Lydia and Dannie around the house. An ice box, which Dad had bought at auction, stood near the washhouse door. Mom was going to buy ice to put in it to keep their food cool during summer.

One morning the children began playing with the ice box. They took out the shelves and found that there was enough room for one of them to sit inside. Then the other two closed the door for a little while. They were careful not to slam it hard enough so it would latch and they didn't keep it shut too long. It was thrilling to sit for a moment in that dark place!

Once, however, when it was Sammie's turn, Lydia slammed the door too hard and it latched. She tried to open it but it was stuck. She couldn't make it work!

At first Sammie didn't realize what had happened. He sat in the dark and waited for Lydia and Dannie to open the door. It didn't open. He pushed against it. It didn't move. He pushed again, harder this time, but it still wouldn't budge. Breathing was becoming difficult. He brought his hand up before his face, but he couldn't see it because it was totally dark. He didn't have much room and could only stay in one position. Panic seized him and he yelled as loud as he could! He pushed against the door again. Nothing did any good! Finally he gave up and simply sat there struggling for breath.

Finally, the door opened and there stood Mom. Sammie tumbled out gasping. He lay on the grass and puffed. Gradually his head cleared and he felt Mom's hands rubbing his back. She set him up.

"Are you okay?" she asked.

Sammie was still breathing hard. He nodded.

"You children stay away from that thing!" Mom ordered, and then sat back on the steps and took a deep breath. Her shoulders sagged and her face was white. She put her hands over her face and sat there for a few minutes before going back into the kitchen.

Sammie didn't understand why it had affected her so.

At noon Mom told Dad what had happened. "I still feel weak all over," she said. "I won't rest until that thing is put away. To think what could have happened!"

After dinner Dad explained it to the children. "If no one had opened the door for you, you could have smothered to death," Dad said quietly. "You must never sit in anything that is airtight. It is dangerous."

Sammie hadn't thought about that. It was a scary thought. No one would have to worry about him playing in anything like that again!

That evening Orin Graber and his son, Allen, came by. They helped Dad carry the ice box into the wash-house, where Mom washed it out and put food in it. That way no one would be tempted to play with it again.

Dad was very busy working in the fields. Every day he hurried away from breakfast and dinner to go back to his work, and every day he stayed out until late, leaving Mom and Sammie to do the chores. One day, however, a man from the canning factory came by, and Dad let the horses stand in the field while they talked. They talked a long time, and, by the time the man left, Dad had signed a contract to raise five acres of tomatoes.

"It doesn't sound like a bad deal," he told Mom when he came into the house afterward. "We raise the tomatoes and the company furnishes the pickers and hauls them to market."

"Yes, it does sound good," Mom said. "When we raised tomatoes at home, we had to do all the picking. I picked so many tomatoes that I didn't care if I ever saw another one."

"Well, that guy seemed to know what he is talking about. I told him we don't have help to do the picking. He told me not to worry. The company will take care of that part," Dad replied.

"Let's see," Dad mused, writing on a piece of paper. "If we could raise six tons of tomatoes per acre at, let's say-a-at twenty dollars a ton. That should come out pretty good." He finished writing the figures with a pleased look on his face.

"Let's not count our chicks before they hatch," Mom reminded him.

"Yes, I know," Dad answered. But he still had that pleased look as he went whistling out the door to his way back to work.

The pasture and hay fields were nice and green now. The sun shone warm and lots of plants grew up out of the earth. Mom said it was time to make dandelion gravy. She took a bowl and a paring knife and went looking. When she came back, she had a bowl of tender young dandelion leaves.

She washed and sorted and chopped the leaves, and set them in a drainer on the sink. Next she made some good brown pan gravy and to this added some vinegar, salt and bits of bacon. Just before serving, she added the chopped up dandelion greens so that they would stay as crisp as possible.

For supper they had mashed potatoes and dandelion gravy. Mom's brown pan gravy was delicious on its own, but her dandelion gravy was better yet. Sammie ate and ate until he was full and he felt good inside.

Now Dad was seeding the oat field. He hitched Queen to the hack, piled it high with bags of oat seed, and drove it to the field. Sammie and Lydia helped watch Queen and the hack while Dad hitched Mollie and Dollie to the seeder and went back and forth planting the oats. Every round Sammie drove Queen ahead to keep up so that Dad never had to walk very far to get seed.

Lydia got tired of sitting and went back to the house. But not Sammie, oh my, no! He would not miss a chance to drive Queen! He sat lazily on the seat and looked across the field. The freshly worked soil was smooth and brown. The barley and hay fields, and the pasture and the grasses along the fence row, stood out fresh and green.

A flock of blackbirds was feeding on the bare oat field. When Dad and the horses got too close, the birds suddenly flew up and found another spot. A whirlwind picked up some dust and dry grass and spun them around and around as it went speeding across the field.

The sun was shining warmly, but a bank of clouds stood in the southwest. Every once in awhile Dad looked in that direction and hurried on. It was chore time when

Dad finished the seeding, and by that time, it looked very much like it was going to rain.

"A good warm rain would give the oats an early start," Dad said, eyeing the clouds.

It was raining by the time they returned to the house after finishing chores. Sammie was glad because Dad had said rain would help make a good crop.

Because the ground was wet, Dad took the time to catch up on work around the barn. Mom was ready to begin planting her garden, and so, as soon as the soil dried she asked Dad, "Could you work up the garden? Soon you will be in the fields again and we won't want to take the horses out of field work when the weather is good."

"I suppose I could," Dad said, and headed for the barn. On the way, he stopped at the garden to check the soil, which he had plowed earlier in the spring, but which still had to be harrowed.

"Yes, it should be okay," he said.

So he hitched Mollie and Dollie to the harrow and prepared the garden soil for planting. When he finished, Mom came out of the house with a box of seeds.

Sammie and Lydia helped Mom do the planting. Mom sowed the carrot, lettuce, radish, and beet seeds. Sammie knew how to plant peas, so he did that with Lydia's help, and then he and Lydia planted some early sweet corn while Mom set out the cabbage plants and cut the potato sets. At first it was fun, but after a while the children grew tired of it.

"My back hurts," Lydia complained.

"I wish we were done," Sammie said.

"We are almost done, children. Let's keep it up," Mom urged.

Dad came and made the potato rows because they had to be extra deep. Then the children planted potatoes while Mom did the onion sets.

Sammie thought his back would break, but he knew he had to keep going. He placed a potato set in the row and stepped on it. Then he went a little more than the length of his foot and planted another. So on he went until they were done, and it seemed like a very long time.

Mom was in a hurry to get her early planting done because she wanted to go visit Grandfather and Grandmother in Tennessee. For a whole week she and Lydia and Dannie and Baby David were going away. Sammie wanted to go too, but he would have to stay home and be Dad's helper.

Chapter 14

Mom's Vacation

The next day Mom was busy packing suitcases for herself and the three younger children to prepare for their trip to Tennessee. By evening everything was ready. They were all set to get on the train the next forenoon.

The morning was filled with excitement. Mom was heating water to give a quick bath to Lydia, Dannie and Baby David and telling Dad and Sammie where to find all the food.

"Remember to water the flowers every other day," she reminded them.

But Sammie had a headache all morning. He sat around and didn't say much.

"What is wrong, Sammie?" Mom asked.

She looked at him in a funny way and came closer.

"What in the world!" she exclaimed, "You have the chicken pox!"

She looked under his clothes. There was no mistake. Sammie really had chicken pox. If he had chicken pox, that meant that Lydia and Dannie and Baby David could get it, too. A trip to Tennessee was out of the question!

Mom got the suitcase and slowly began unpacking. She said nothing, but the muscles on her face were taut and she did not seem like Mom at all. Then suddenly she looked up and said, "Well, no sense brooding. What can't be changed must be accepted."

"Chicken pox doesn't last forever," Dad said then. "Maybe the trip can be made later."

"We'll see," Mom answered. With that, she began humming a tune and went about her work as usual.

For two days Sammie felt sick. He didn't mind staying in the house then. But after that he felt as good as new. If it hadn't been for the pimples all over his body, he would have forgotten about the chicken pox. He wanted to go out and play, but Mom said no.

"You better stay inside and hold still for a few days," she said. "I don't want you to get a back set."

"What is a back set?" Sammie asked.

"That is when you get sick again before you are over a disease. And the second time is usually worse than the first," Mom explained.

A few days later, Sammie complained, "I'm tired of staying inside! I want to go out now!"

Mom looked at him thinking. "Would you like to go out on the porch for a while?" she asked.

Sammie nodded. Anything was better than staying cooped up in the house.

"Okay," Mom concluded, "Hold still and it shouldn't do any harm."

The world had changed while Sammie was in the house. It was now the first week in May and the woods to the south were turning green fast. The oak tree was putting forth leaves. Here and there on the lawn were yellow dandelion blossoms.

A robin was hopping about looking for food and a squirrel was scolding in the tree. It was nice to be outside and to see all these things, but very soon Sammie was tired of looking. He wanted something to do.

There was a clothesline strung from one end of the porch to the other and he began swinging on it. He took hold with both hands, leaned back, and gave himself a push. He lifted up his feet and away he went back and forth. It was great fun until suddenly, BANG! The nail that held the clothesline to the wall pulled loose, and Sammie hurtled to the floor, striking his head on the corner of a post.

It really hurt. He let out a scream, then tried hard not to cry, because he didn't want Mom to see what had happened. But she had already heard him and had come quickly to see what was the matter.

"My, my! What did you do?" she asked.

Sammie was holding his head, and hurting too much to answer. Mom looked around.

"Sammie," she chided, "Were you swinging on the clothesline?"

Sammie nodded through his tears. He felt very naughty, and expected Mom to say more, and maybe even spank him.

Mom's mouth opened ready to speak, then closed again. She looked at his head. There was a big bump where he had struck the post. She looked at it closer and said it was quite an ugly knob.

She led him into the kitchen and made him sit on a chair while she took her scissors and snipped the hair from the area.

Lydia and Dannie stood around watching sympathetically and exclaimed at the great bump. It still hurt, but all the attention made him feel quite important. It wasn't every day that someone had a great big bump on his head.

Mom put some butter on it and said it would probably be okay in a day or so, and it was. As Sammie began to get better, each of the other children experienced the same childhood "rite of passage" and kept Mom busy nursing them back to health. After they all were over the chicken pox, however, Mom again began planning a trip to Tennessee. It was a busier time, because all of the garden was planted by now and had to be weeded, and the lawn, which was growing very rapidly, had to be cut every week. Mom wanted all those things done before she left and, because Dad was busy farming, she either had to do them or make sure somebody else did.

But the day finally came. The suitcases were repacked and everything made ready. They were going to get on the train in the night. They all went to bed as usual, but knew that in a few hours they'd be up and heading for the depot.

That night, Orin Graber came knocking on the door to report that his father, who lived at their house, had died from a heart attack. So the trip to Tennessee would have to be postponed again.

The children couldn't see why the death of Orin Graber's father should keep them from going, but Mom said. "When things like this happen in the community, you drop what you are doing and go help. God wants us to help each other, and the neighbors would do the same for us. Do you remember last fall when we had a frolic? All the neighbors left their work and came to help us."

The children remembered the frolic and they remembered many other times when neighbors had come to help them, like on butchering day and when they were preparing to have church at their house.

But this time Mom didn't unpack the bags. She just set them aside and hurried with the work. For each of the three days until the funeral, Dad went to help and provide comfort to the family in the morning. At noon he came home and Mom went in the afternoon.

After the funeral was over, Mom and the little ones again began preparing to go on their vacation.

"I wonder what will come up now to keep us from going," Mom said, "They say 'if it happens twice, it happens thrice'."

But the saying, fortunately, didn't hold true this time. In the night Mom got the children out of bed and helped them into their clothes. At first they were sleepy, but then they remembered that they were actually going away, and became wide awake.

Dad hitched Queen to the buggy, everyone got on, and off they went to the train depot. It was a small depot and there weren't many people around. Mom and Lydia and Dannie and Baby David settled down on the chairs to wait, and Sammie went out on the platform with Dad to watch for the train.

The night was still, and millions of tiny stars glittered in the dark sky. Suddenly from far away came the lonely sound of the train whistle. In a few minutes it came again and then they could see the single headlight piercing the blackness.

Mom and the children hurried out to the platform, and the ticket agent came out carrying a lantern. He stood on the tracks and waved the lantern back and forth until the train began slowing down. In a moment the giant humming engines passed by and the cars went slower and slower until the train came to a complete stop.

Quickly two men in red caps grabbed Mom's baggage and loaded it. Dad helped with the children and stood by the door until Mom was settled in a seat. In a short time the door closed and the train began moving again.

Sammie had been excited with all the commotion, but now he stood thinking. They wouldn't see Mom and the little children for a whole week. The wheels were picking up speed and clackety-clacked along before him but

Sammie had lost interest in the train. He wished Mom and the children hadn't gone.

Soon the last car disappeared into the black night, and left Sammie with an enormous empty feeling. Dad reached down and took Sammie's hand in his.

"Come, Sammie, let's go home," he said.

The little farm seemed strange without Mom and the other children there, and time passed slowly. Nobody came out to tell them it was dinner time. There was no Baby David fussing to be fed when they came in. Dad and Sammie had to get the food on the table and there was no one to quarrel with about whose turn it was to wipe dishes.

Dad wasn't much of a cook. He did know how to make good egg sandwiches, though, so they ate a lot of them while Mom was gone. Of course there were jars of peaches and pears and apple sauce in the root cellar, and Mom had baked some cookies, some halfmoon pies and a cake for them. But almost every meal had egg sandwiches in it.

Dad laughed and said, "Today we'll eat egg sandwiches and fruit. Then tomorrow for a change, we'll have fruit and egg sandwiches!"

Allen Graber came across the fields mornings and nights to help with chores. Allen wasn't like Freeman and Abner. Sammie liked him, and Dad said he was a good worker. Once he put Sammie on his shoulders and gave him a fast ride through the barn. It was fun to have Allen around and it helped the time to pass more quickly.

The day after Mom left, Sammie tramped into a nail with his bare foot. He sat right down and looked at it. The pain had been sharp when the nail went in, but now the wound looked very small and it didn't hurt much. He went on all day and didn't think much about it, but by chore time his foot was very sore and he was limping badly.

"What is wrong with your foot?" Dad asked at milking time.

"I stepped on a nail," Sammie answered.

Dad took a look at it. The wound was red and swollen.

"I'm afraid you'll get an infection in there," he said. "After chores we'll have to do something about that."

Usually Mom took care of the wounds and the hurts, and Sammie wished she were home. But Dad knew what to do, too. He went to the corner of the garden next to the rhubarb bed where there was a little patch of tansy, broke off a handful of tansy leaves, and steeped them in boiling water. As soon as the tansy water had cooled enough, Sammie stuck his foot in it. It was still too hot to keep his foot in for long, so he pulled it back out. But a little at a time he held the foot in the tansy water until it was cool enough to keep it in and then he soaked it for a long time. Afterwards the foot felt much better.

After the soaking was finished, Dad put some salve on the wound and tied a strip of white cloth around the foot. The next morning it was still sore but didn't throb like it had in the evening. Sammie soaked his foot again and Dad put more salve on and bound it up.

"Be careful you don't get any dirt in it," Dad told him.

Day after day it got better, and, when it was time for Mom to come home, he was hardly limping at all.

Then Sammie was all over excited! Mom was coming home! Dad hitched Queen to the buggy and they drove to the station and waited. It was different than when Mom and the children had left. It was the middle of the day, and the sun shone brightly. The train whistle didn't sound nearly as lonesome this time!

The train came in, going slower and slower until it finally stopped. Mom stepped from the car onto the platform. She had Baby David in one arm and a bag in the other. Lydia and Dannie followed close behind. The porter put the suitcases on the platform, and in a moment they were all together and walking back to the buggy. Dad carried the suitcases, Mom carried Baby David, and Sammie held on to Lydia and Dannie's hands. Everyone was laughing and trying to talk at once. Sammie tried to tell the others about stepping on a nail and about his ride on Allen's shoulder and about the new calf that was born while they were gone, but no one was listening because they were all talking, too.

Finally when they were all seated in the buggy heading for home, Dad said, "Children, be quiet. After all, we can listen to only one person at a time. Let Mom tell her story first. After that there will be plenty of time for the rest of you to talk. When everyone speaks at once, it just sounds like a bunch of chickens."

The rest of the way home they all listened while Mom talked about the trip. She told them about how the people in Tennessee were already eating fresh vegetables from the garden. She talked about the cotton fields and the pepper fields and the strawberry patches and the beautiful wooded hills.

Lydia and Dannie had earned a few pennies by helping pull weeds in Grandfather's cotton field, and Dannie also had three pieces of candy in his pocket. A neighbor of Grandfather's had given Dannie one big piece of candy, but he dropped it on the floor and it broke into three pieces. The man had quickly gathered the pieces up and explained to Dannie that things weren't as bad as they seemed, because now there were three pieces of candy instead of one. So Dannie had quit crying and was quite happy with the treat.

When they arrived home, Mom opened the suitcases. Grandfather and Grandmother had sent gifts for everyone.

They had remembered Sammie, too, and sent him a book of nursery rhymes. It was full of witty verses and beautiful pictures, and Grandmother had written his name inside the front cover.

There was a rhyme about a small girl named Mary who had a little lamb. Another one was about a Little Boy Blue who went to sleep by the haystack and let the cows get into the cornfield. That was a favorite to Sammie.

Then, because he had stayed home and helped Dad while the rest went on vacation, Mom had brought him a little toy car with a friction motor! What a treat! Sammie was glad he had stayed home. He pushed the car until the wheels were spinning. Then he put it on the floor and watched it speeding across the living room.

Now Mom looked around the house. Next she looked at the clock.

"Well, it is time to get back to work!" she said. "Children, can you help me put these clothes away in their places?"

Sammie and Lydia helped, and they quickly had everything put away. After that Mom took out an everyday apron and put it on over her dark blue Sunday dress. She hurried through the house and began putting things in order.

She watered the flowers on the window sill right away, because they looked dry. There were dishes to wash and many things were out of place. A week without Mom in the kitchen had really made a difference!

Soon things looked like normal again and Mom set to work making an early supper. She sent Sammie and Lydia to the root cellar after canned things, and, after a while, they all sat down to Mom's good cooking. She had mashed potatoes and gravy and canned beef and peas and applesauce and peaches. There was no bread because they had eaten it all up while Mom was gone, but they didn't mind. Dad and Sammie enjoyed the good food like never before and it was nice to be together again.

After supper the children eagerly ran with Dad to help with the chores.

"I think I could milk a cow," Sammie told Dad stretching himself to his full height.

Dad looked up from his milking.

"Well, maybe you can," he answered, "Get a bucket and see what you can do with Bessie."

Bessie was one of the older cows. She was very tame and didn't give a lot of milk right now because she was almost dry.

It looked easy when Dad and Mom and Allen Graber milked. They sloshed wide streams into the pail and quickly filled it up. Always they had a good thick layer of foam on top of the milk. That was the way Sammie wanted to milk.

He sat down and began squeezing really fast, but hardly any milk came out. In no time at all his hands were tired, but the pail was still almost empty. He stopped to rest, and Bessie looked back and stepped aside.

"You have to keep at it," Dad said. He was pouring milk into the strainer and watching Sammie, "If you stop, she thinks you want to quit. That is why she steps around."

So Sammie tried again. He gripped the two front teats and squeezed until milk went flowing into the bucket. If he went slowly he could keep it up much better. But he knew it was going to take a long time at this rate.

"I-I guess I can't milk very fast," he said looking at Dad.

Dad studied him a little then said, "You are doing okay. Just keep at it. You'll be surprised at how much easier it is when you get used to it."

So Sammie kept on. It took a long time to milk Bessie and no foam came on top of the milk. Finally he decided she must be done. He carried the milk to the strainer and poured it in. He had actually milked a cow!

Of course Dad had to check to make sure that Bessie was milked out. But when he was done he said, "That was pretty good for the first time, Sammie. Keep it up and you can learn to be a good milker."

Sammie's arms and hands were very tired from milking, and he was disappointed at how long it took, but what Dad said made him feel much better. Soon he would be able to milk fast and he'd have foam on his milk too!

After chores Dad didn't go to the field as he normally would have. He and Mom sat on the front porch and talked. Dannie sat on Dad's lap, Mom held Baby David and Sammie and Lydia sat and listened. Twilight was falling over the land and it was good to be together again. It was the happiest evening they had had for a long time.

Chapter 15

Haymaking Time

Dad had finished the spring planting while Mom and the little ones were in Tennessee. Now the tender young corn plants were poking their way up through the soil, reaching for the warm sun that shone almost every day. The spindly tomato plants stood forlorn and wilted on the bare five-acre field. The weather was dry and it was hard on the young sets. But finally, after a rain, they began growing and Dad said they would be okay.

The cows were on pasture now. Grass grew up fresh and juicy out of the earth. The cows loved new grass. Every day they ate and ate until they were full and their middles were as round as balloons. Then they lay in the shade along the fence row and contentedly chewed their cuds.

Sammie loved to watch them as they shifted their full bodies to let out a belch. Then they swallowed and went on chewing. Twice a day the cows came to the barn to be milked. They gave more milk now and it had a sweet pasture smell.

It was early June, and Dad said it was time to make hay. The red clover was in blossom and the pale green timothy stood tall and straight and waved in the winds.

Dad pushed the hay mower out of the shed. He took out the long cutting sickle and sharpened it, greased the mower and tightened some bolts. Then he hitched up Mollie and Dollie and began cutting hay.

Sammie and Lydia watched as Dad guided the horses around the outside to "open the field." After one round, he turned around and went the other way. Mollie and Dollie walked swiftly, pulling the pur-r-r-ring mower. The sickle went back and forth quickly snip-a-de-snip-snipping down the sweet smelling hay. A smooth swath of timothy and clover mix kept falling over the sickle bar and lay there to be dried in the hot sun.

Sport went bounding excitedly over the field. He was very busy chasing rabbits, mice and birds as they were scared out of the hay by the mower.

Every time Dad came around, a red-wing blackbird scolded and flew at him, fluttering angrily.

"Why does that bird go after you?" Sammie asked when Dad stopped the horses to rest.

"I suppose she has a nest around here someplace," Dad answered, looking around. He got off the mower seat and waded into the hay. He took the nest, which was made from fine grass and horse hair and contained three light blue eggs with tiny dark specks on them, from where it was built on the hay stems.

"Don't breathe into the nest or touch it," Dad warned. "The mother bird will leave it if you do."

He set the nest in the tall grass of the fence row.

"I hope she can find it here. I can't leave it in the hay or it will be spoiled for sure," Dad said.

All the time the red-wing blackbird kept fluttering and scolding, "Check! check! check!"

When Dad went on cutting more birds came. They swiftly glided in toward the mower, then rose quickly and flew away.

"Are those birds scolding you, too?" Sammie asked when Dad stopped again.

"No, those are barn swallows. They are catching insects which are being chased out of the hay. Watch. They eat some now and they take some to their young in the barn," Dad explained.

Now it made more sense to Sammie. The swallows glided in gracefully. They made their catch and flew away with it. On and on they came. Sometimes they passed right between Dad and the horses. Then suddenly they flew straight up and glided away like the wind.

The children got tired of watching Dad work and went back to the barn. After a while, Lydia went into the house, but Sammie stayed in the barn to watch the swallows. It was just as Dad had said. One after another the swallows came into the barn and flew to a nest on the side of a beam. The young swallows made a terrible racket as the adult gave the insect to one of them. Then as Sammie watched, the swallow flew out of the barn and headed straight back to the hay field.

After a while Sammie went back to the hayfield and sat in the fence row to watch Dad. As the mower went toward the far end of the field the purring faded until it could not be heard at all. Sammie sat waiting for his Dad to come around again.

While he waited, he could see the cows contentedly eating grass. The yellow dandelion blossoms were gone now, and in their place were fuzzy white tops sitting up on tall stems. The wild geraniums were blooming in the fence row as were the wild Sweet William and the chamomile.

Birds were singing happily because summer had come. Sammie listened dreamily to the twittering. Above it all he heard the call of the killdeer in the cornfield and the swingy song of the meadowlark across the pasture.

By Sammie's face was a sweet-smelling plant. When he picked some, the aroma became stronger. Soon he heard the mower again, and could see the horses walking along the other side of the field. Dad sat on the mower seat with his right hand on the lever, carefully watching where the sickle bar was cutting, and drove the horses with the other hand. Dad stopped the mower so that the horses could have a rest, and Sammie took some of the sweet smelling plant and showed it to Dad.

"It is a kind of mint," Dad explained. "Go ahead and pick some and take it to the house. It should make good tea."

The next morning for breakfast, Mom made some of that tea and it was good. That day Sammie and Lydia went out and gathered a whole bunch of the mint. Mom put newspaper on the floor of the spare bedroom upstairs and spread it out to dry.

"That way we can have tea later on," Mom explained. "It will taste good next winter!"

Dad was cutting hay again that day. It was very warm and the children had to take water to him in the field. As they rounded the edge of the barn, they heard Dad yell, "Whoa!" much louder than usual. They saw him bending over the sickle bar. When they came closer, they saw Sport lying there whimpering.

"I hit him." Dad said shaking his head, "He was in the hay and I didn't see him."

Sport's left front paw was cut to the bone. At every little movement he whimpered and leaned forward to lick the wound.

"I'm afraid the tendons are cut through," Dad said. He looked around and thought a little, and then said, "Sammie, go get the wheelbarrow."

When Sammie came back, Dad gently laid Sport on the wheelbarrow and slowly wheeled him back to the barn. There he put salve on the wound and wrapped some white cloth around the leg. He chained Sport to the post in the feed alley and went back to cutting hay.

Sammie, Lydia and Dannie stayed and stroked Sport's silky black coat. Every time they began walking away, Sport's brown eyes looked sadly at them and he whimpered. He didn't like being chained, but that couldn't be helped. Whenever he moved his foot he winced in pain and tried to pull off the bandage to lick the wound.

The children felt very sorry for him, so they stayed with him as much as possible. After dinner, when they came out, he had the bandage pulled off. Dad put on more salve and bandaged it again, but by chore time that evening the bandage was off again.

"Okay," Dad said, "we'll leave it off. I suppose we'll have to chain Sport whenever we cut hay. I can't figure out why dogs don't stay away from the sickle."

The next day they began hauling hay. Dad said it was dry when he came in for dinner. He had raked it on smooth long windrows as soon as the dew was gone that morning.

"Can I get a helper to drive the horses?" Dad asked looking at Sammie.

Sammie had never before driven the horses for the haying, and it sounded very exciting.

After dinner Dad hitched Mollie and Dollie to the wagon and drove around the barn. The tall hay-loader stood along the fence behind the barn. Dad pulled on the lines and the horses steadily backed until the loader could be hooked on.

Dad drove to the hay field and the loader came trailing along behind. He guided the horses to the first windrow and stopped. He jumped from the wagon and went to the hub of the loader. On each side was a little lever that had to be flipped to put the loader in gear. Now they were ready to make hay.

Sammie stood on the front wagon rack and took the lines. Dad grabbed the pitchfork and stood on the wagon bed.

"Okay!" he said, and he clucked to start the horses.

Sammie held the lines tightly because Dad wanted the horses to walk slowly. He kept his eyes on Mollie and Dollie's broad backs with the driving lines curving down to their heads. He watched the windrow disappear under the front end of the wagon.

He knew that the hooks on the loader's cylinder were picking up the hay and smoothly passing it to the web which elevated it to the wagon. But he didn't look back. It was important to keep Dollie walking on one side of the windrow and Mollie on the other.

The horses walked slowly across the field. The loader picked up the hay and moved it to the top, then dropped it into the wagon. Dad gathered pitchfork after pitchfork-full of hay and spread it evenly. He knew just where to put each forkful and in the end he always had a good, solid square-looking load.

When the wagon was full, Sammie stopped the horses. Dad unhooked the loader and drove to the barn. He guided Mollie and Dollie into the driveway beside the haymow and unhitched them.

"Can you drive to pull up the hay, too?" Dad asked.

Sammie didn't know. That looked quite a bit harder.

"Well, I'll drive the first time," Dad said then.

He climbed up on the wagon and stuck the four grapple hooks into the load. Then Dad jumped back down and hooked the horses' traces to the double-tree fastened to the hook at the end of the large hay rope.

Dad clucked, and the horses walked out the driveway toward the road. The rope ran through the pulleys drawing on the grapple hooks as they gathered a bunch of hay and moved it upward and swung it into the mow.

"Whoa!" Dad yelled that very instant. He let the horses stand and came back to trip the hooks. He pulled on a little rope and "WHOOOSH!" the bunch of hay dropped to the mow below.

"Do you think you can drive the next time?" Dad asked then.

"I don't know," Sammie said doubtfully.

"Come," Dad said. He took a piece of board and placed it where the horses' front feet were. "When you get to this spot, you stop."

That made it easier. Dad again stuck the hooks into the load of hay, and Sammie drove the horses toward the board. At the very instant when they came to the board, Sammie heard Dad yell, "WHOA!". Almost at the same time he heard that bunch of hay fall to the mow with another big, "WHOOSH," followed by a tinkle as the hooks swung back into the idle position.

Sammie turned Mollie and Dollie around and drove them back to the barn. He was happy that everything had worked right. It gave him more confidence, and the unloading went on smoothly. Sammie walked behind the horses and did the driving and Dad worked the hooks and spread the hay in the mow. When the wagon was empty, they went to the field for another load.

All afternoon they hauled hay. The next day they hauled hay and the next after that. In the evenings, they were very tired. Every night Sammie dragged himself up the stairs and flopped into bed. In a minute he was fast asleep. The next morning he was still tired. But again Dad raked hay and the hauling had to go on.

"You have to make hay while the sun shines," Dad said.

As long as there was hay on the ground drying, the work couldn't stop. Dry weather doesn't last forever, and rain on dry hay spoils it. That's what Dad said.

"Can't you dry it after the rain?" Sammie asked.

"Yes, you can," Dad answered then, "but the stock won't eat it as well, and the high feed value is gone."

So Dad and Mom always watched the weather signs during haymaking. As long as the sun went down clear and red in the evening and came up gray in the morning, all was well.

"Red at night, sailors' delight. Red in the morning, sailors' warning," Mom always said.

On the evening of the third day the sun slid down behind a low wall of gray clouds.

"That spells other weather," Mom declared.

"Well, if we have one more good day, we can finish the haying," Dad said. "Hopefully wet weather will hold off that long."

Chapter 16

Summer Storm

On the fourth morning, Dad and Mom and Sammie were up before the sun. The eastern sky was ablaze with deep red streaks. The sun sent glowing colors out on every side until they changed to a deep purple and finally joined the blue-gray morning sky. There was hardly any dew, so the haymaking could start early.

Sammie was still tired from the day before. His muscles ached and he wished he didn't have to go back to haying.

"I think we can finish today if the weather holds," Dad said as they milked the cows. "It is a good thing that I have a willing helper."

Sammie looked at Dad's eyes twinkling at him. Already his muscles felt better and his tiredness seemed to melt away.

The day was more humid and warmer that any of the previous days had been. Before noon sweat was already standing on Sammie's forehead as he stood on the wagon rack driving Mollie and Dollie. Dad's shirt was soaked, but he kept gathering forkful after forkful of dry hay and placing them carefully on the wagon to form a good solid load.

Mom had made some mint tea and put it in the cooling tank in the milk-house. After every load they stopped and got a drink of good, cool, refreshing tea.

At noon, clouds were bunching up on the southwest. Dad and Sammie hurried away from the dinner table and went back to hauling hay.

The sun beat down warmer than ever, and Dad told Sammie to drive faster. The hay came onto the wagon faster and Dad worked swiftly to keep it from bunching up in the front of the loader. He placed the hay evenly on the wagon and tramped it down as he went. Sweat stood on his forehead and ran down the side of his face. Still he kept on. When the load was as full as others before, Dad continued to add more. Finally he told Sammie to stop. It was a very tall load of hay.

Dad wiped the sweat from his face with his wet handkerchief. Quickly he unhooked the loader and waded through the hay to the front of the wagon. He took the lines from Sammie and drove to the barn. Sammie lay back into the soft hay resting. The load bounced gently up and down and he paid no attention to where they were going until they were almost to the barn. He saw the barn door opening loom up ahead and started to get to his feet.

"Get down, Sammie!" Dad ordered.

Sammie ducked down. It was a tall load of hay and it reached almost to the beam overhead. Dad bent down, too, but Sammie saw the beam catch his shoulders and push him into the hay. When they were inside the barn, he saw that Dad had hurt his back and was wincing in pain.

The rain was coming and there was still more hay to be hauled, but Dad could not go on with his back hurting like that. So he and Sammie went to the house.

"My, my! What happened?" Mom exclaimed. She got the liniment bottle from the medicine cabinet and rubbed Dad's sore back.

"Maybe you had better quit making hay for the day," she said.

"No, I'll be okay in a bit," Dad answered.

"Are you sure?" she asked.

He got up from his chair wincing a little, "Yes, I can manage now. That liniment helped," he said.

He and Sammie went back out and slowly unloaded the hay.

"There's about two more loads," Dad said when they headed for the field again. He kept watching toward the southwest. The clouds were higher now. The sun was gone and the air was unusually still. When they stopped to hook on the loader, they heard a low rumble of thunder.

Sammie guided the horses to the windrow and again they began loading hay. The storm was coming fast, but they couldn't hurry. Dad slowly pitched the hay, first to one corner, then to another, then along the sides. Finally he filled up the middle and tramped it down.

Sammie couldn't hear the thunder above the noise of the loader, but lightning zig-zagged between heaven and earth and dark clouds were rolling overhead now. He felt a drop of rain on his cheek. Next several cool drops pelted his arm, and a wall of rain was speeding across the field toward them.

"Whoa!" Dad called, He started to unhook the loader, but changed his mind. The rain was pattering down fast.

"Run for the house!" he shouted above the sound of the storm.

Sammie jumped from the wagon and ran! He looked back to see Dad unhooking the horses. He gave them a slap and let them go. They ran toward the buildings, and Dad was coming, too.

Mollie and Dollie ran past Sammie and stopped by the chicken house. They stood with backs hunched on the side away from the storm.

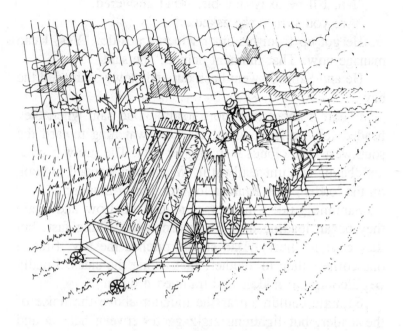

Sammie ran on to the house gasping for breath. Mom was holding the door open, and he ran on in. He stood dripping on the rug inside the door, soaked from head to toe.

"Where's Dad?" Mom asked anxiously.

"He's coming," Sammie answered. He expected Dad to come bursting in the door at any moment, but he didn't.

The storm now came with renewed fury! Thunder cracked and lightning flashed. The house trembled and the windows rattled as the rain pounded against them.

Lydia and Dannie started to cry.

"Don't cry children," Mom said, gathering them in her arms. "God can see us here. He'll care for us."

They stopped crying and stood fearfully by Mom's side. She dried their tears with her apron.

"I wonder where Dad is." Sammie said walking toward the window.

"Come back from the window, Sammie!" Mom ordered. "Never go near a window when there's lightning."

Gradually the storm lessened. It was still raining, but the wind did not blow as hard, and the thunder was reduced to low rumbling in the distance. Sammie looked out the window, but Dad was nowhere in sight. He went to the living room and looked out toward the road.

"Mom, come here!" he called.

Small twigs and leaves were strewn all over the yard. A car was stopped by the mailbox, apparently waiting for the storm to pass. But the real sight was a pigeon sitting on the ground under the oak tree. It stood drawn together, braving the rain.

"Poor thing!" Mom said. "The storm must have come up so fast that it did not have time to make it to the barn."

Soon the car went on down the road. The rain had almost stopped. The pigeon shook the water from her feathers and flew away.

Sammie ran back to the kitchen window. He was just in time to see Dad crawling out of one of the A-frame hog shanties west of the barn.

"WHEW!" Dad whistled when he came in. He stood dripping on the throw rug just inside the door.

Mom looked at his soaked clothes and laughed, but then she said, "For a while I wished we had gone to the root cellar."

"I figured you probably had," Dad answered, "It sounded pretty bad in that flimsy little hog shanty."

"Is everything okay outside?" Mom asked.

"I can't see anything wrong here, but there is a tree down in Harold's yard. I suppose there's more damage around the country the way the wind blew," Dad said.

"Oh well," Mom said, "It is over now. There is much to be thankful for EVEN if some of the hay got wet."

"It isn't all that much, probably two loads. When it dries again, we'll put it up for the horses. What they don't eat, we'll throw over for bedding," Dad said.

Mom hurried to get some dry clothes. Sammie put on his and they felt clean and soft.

Dad's back still hurt so Mom rubbed it again with liniment. The children went out to play. Sammie and Dannie rolled up their pant legs and Lydia lifted her skirt as they waded through the large puddles.

Soon Dad came out. Mollie and Dollie still stood by the chicken house where they had gone for shelter during the storm, so he drove them to the barn and put them in their stalls.

It had cooled off, and the air smelled fresh and clean. Mud oozed up between the children's toes as they walked over the wet earth. Then they ran through the puddles and washed it off.

After supper and chores, Sammie got out the little red wagon. He kneeled on it with one leg and pushed himself with the other. Around the driveway and through the puddles he went. He liked to look back and see the waves that each wheel created spread out until they were gone.

Finally he stopped and just sat on the wagon. He was tired. But the wet and coolness had brought a welcome change from the hot weather and haymaking. It would get dark early, because it was cloudy. A fog was gathering in the lowlands along the Salamonie River.

There was already a light in the kitchen. Sammie could see Mom standing by the window washing dishes. Her clear voice carried to where he was sitting as she sang the song,

"HOW GREAT THOU ART"

Oh, Lord, my God when I in awesome wonder,
Consider all the works Thy hands have made;
I see the stars, I hear the mighty thunder,
Thy power throughout the universe displayed.
Then sings my soul, my Savior God to Thee
How great Thou art, how great Thou art!
Then sings my soul, my Savior God to Thee
How great Thou art, how great Thou art!

It was a peaceful evening and Sammie was happy even if he was tired. Suddenly a mosquito bit him on the arm. He slapped at it and soon there was another. The dampness of the evening was bringing them out. It was time to go into the house.

Chapter 17

Summertime

The wet weather brought a stop to the haymaking, which was good, because Dad's back still hurt.

"A few days of rest should make it good as new," Dad said cheerfully.

But to Dad resting didn't mean sitting around doing nothing. It only meant that he didn't have to go on with a hard job like haying.

"Change of work is resting," he often said.

There were lots of odd jobs around the little farm waiting to be done. The chicken house roof needed mending, there was always fence to fix, Queen needed new shoes, harnesses had to be mended, plus Mom had a list of things around the house to be done.

But on the morning after the storm Dad didn't do any of those things. He got the ladder from the shed and slung a piece of rope over his shoulder. The children followed him to the front yard wondering what he was going to do.

In a minute they had it figured out and jumped up and down with joy! He was making a swing!

He set up the ladder against a stout branch of the old oak tree. He then took one end of the rope, climbed up, and securely fastened it to the branch. Next he pulled up the other end and tied that also, leaving the rope hanging low enough so the children could sit on the bottom end of the loop and swing back and forth. Dad took the ladder back to the shed. He found a piece of board about a foot long and, with his saw, cut little notches out of both ends. Now he brought it to the tree and placed it on the rope. The rope fit into the notches and kept the board from falling off, making a nice seat for the swing.

Now it was done and the children could have rides. But they must always remember to be unselfish and not quarrel about it. If they took turns and played nicely, they could have lots of fun, Dad told them.

"Turn-about is fair play," he said.

That afternoon Dad fixed the roof of the chicken house. Sammie climbed up the ladder and watched. When he was climbing back down, he missed his step and fell down, banging his knee against the bottom rung of the ladder. It hurt and he cried.

Dad came down to see what was wrong. He looked at the knee and said, "It should heal before the cat lays an egg. I suppose you should have stayed off the ladder. Take a lesson from it."

That was what Dad and Mom always said when a hurt didn't amount to very much. Sammie knew that a cat would never lay an egg, so any hurt would not have any trouble beating that deadline!

The next morning the knee was better, and he ran and played again as he had before.

That day Dad fixed fence. He hitched Tim, the all-purpose horse, to the hack, backed the hack up to the shed, and loaded his fence repairing tools and supplies on it. Then he and Sammie got up on the seat, ready to go. Before Dad could get the lines unwrapped, Tim started off with a such a hard jerk that both Dad and Sammie lost their balance. The seat, which wasn't fastened to the hack bed, went flying over backwards, and Dad and Sammie and the seat all landed in a tangled heap among the fence supplies!

"WHOA!" Dad yelled loudly.

It was a good thing that Tim knew what "whoa" meant and stopped immediately. Dad and Sammie picked themselves up. Sammie didn't think it was funny, but Dad laughed a little.

"I guess I'm too used to Queen. She waits to start until I tell her," Dad said.

Dad got some tools and screws from the shop and fastened the hack seat securely to the bed. "There, that should hold it," he said when he had finished.

They started out again, and this time, Dad made sure he had the lines before Tim took off. The seat was solid and secure and stayed in place as they drove to the field, Sport tagging along behind.

Sport's paw still wasn't healed. It dangled pitifully and he could not put any weight on it. Later when it did heal, it became stiff and Sport limped for the rest of his life. But that didn't stop Sport. As soon as they unsnapped his chain, he was outside and following Dad around the farm. He hopped around on three legs and seemed as happy as before.

That day while Dad fixed fence, Sammie found a washout in the pasture. It was as deep as Sammie was tall, and, at the very bottom of it, the rains had washed some clean sand. Sammie played there until Dad was finished with the fence.

The next day Sammie, Lydia and Dannie took some toys and again went there. Sammie had his little horses and wagon, plus other farm animals from the toy box. He built little roads and made small hills and with sticks he built a house and barn. From the fence row he got some branches and stuck them in the sand for toy trees.

When Mom called them in for dinner, they quickly left their play and went back to the house. "Let's leave the toys here," Sammie suggested. "Yes, let's." Lydia agreed, "Right after dinner we can come back and play some more."

But after dinner, Mom had some work for Lydia, and Dannie had to take his afternoon nap. Sammie forgot all about playing in the washout.

Later that afternoon as Sammie and Dad were walking through the pasture, they came to the washout. Suddenly Dad stopped short and looked sharply down to where the children had been playing that morning.

"I-yi-yi, look down there!" Dad whispered hoarsely. He picked up Sammie under the armpits and lifted him so he could see.

Down in the washout with the toys was a large snake. It was coiled up and its shiny black skin glistened in the sun. Sammie was close enough to see its beady eyes and its thin tongue flicking quickly back and forth.

"It is a blue racer," Dad quietly said as he let Sammie back down.

Sammie stood back a ways and watched while Dad got a stick from the fence row, cautiously went down into the washout, and swiftly and surely killed the snake. For a moment Sammie couldn't see him, but then Dad appeared, carrying the dead snake draped over the stick.

"It is a good five feet long," Dad said stretching it out on the pasture. Sport showed his teeth and growled. He circled around and wouldn't go near.

Dad helped Sammie pick up all the toys and take them back to the house. "I don't think you'll want to play down there again," Dad said. Sammie shook his head. Just thinking about it made goose pimples come out all over his arm.

By now the warm sun had again dried the land. Little spikes of corn had pushed through the soil, the little green leaves had spread out, and the plants were growing nicely. But the weeds grew, too. Button weed, red-root pigweed, milkweed, lambs' quarters, yellow dock and fox tail grass had all sprung up and were trying to smother out the corn. So Dad had to hurry with his cultivation to keep ahead of the weeds.

Dad rode on the seat of the sulky cultivator with his feet on the guiding peddles. The shovels dug into the soil, dislodging the little weeds and throwing fine dirt around the little corn plants. The horses had to walk slowly and Dad had to guide the cultivator carefully, or corn plants would get covered up too. When that happened, he stopped and uncovered the plant with a stick he carried for that purpose.

When Sammie walked along behind, he could clear the dirt away from the young corn plants for Dad. Dad said it was a great help and very important. "Every little corn plant means an ear of corn next fall," he said.

So Sammie followed behind, watching under the cultivator. Sometimes he missed a plant. When he did, Dad stopped and told him where it was. He pushed aside the soil and sure enough, there was a little corn plant.

Sammie loved to feel the soft, freshly worked ground under his bare toes. Cultivating corn was a quiet job, and they could hear the birds twittering and singing. Once a killdeer scolded and ran frantically back and forth when they came to a certain spot in the field. Dad stopped the horses and found the killdeer's nest.

Sammie was surprised. He would never have found it. It looked so much like the ground around it. There was just a little dip in the earth and the nest was lined with a few little round stones and sticks. The two speckled eggs blended perfectly into the surroundings.

When Dad came to the nest, he took the cultivator shovels out of the ground and passed over it. The mother killdeer screamed and scolded. She flew a short distance, then came down acting like she was hurt.

"She does that to draw us away from the nest," Dad explained.

"Don't worry," Sammie thought to himself, "your nest is safe." He was happy that it hadn't been disturbed.

It took a long time to cultivate the corn, and Sammie got tired of following behind. Twenty-three acres was a lot of corn to a little boy!

While Dad worked in the fields, Mom was busy around the house. She had to care for the garden and clean the flowerbeds, plus there was the normal washing, ironing, mending, cleaning and cooking meals. But when Eli Mullets had church at their house, she found time to go help them get ready.

Sammie, Lydia, Dannie, and Baby David all got to go along. They went in the morning and stayed the whole day.

Sammie was looking forward to spending a day with Oley, but it didn't turn out the way he had planned. Almost before they started playing, they got into a quarrel which spoiled the whole visit.

A few days before, Eli had received a new batch of baby turkeys. When Mom and the children arrived that morning, Oley was helping his Dad. They were trying to get the young birds to eat.

"Turkey's are the most stupid birds," Eli explained to Sammie. "It beats me out, but they can starve to death with feed right in front of their nose."

Already there was a pile of dead baby turkeys outside the enclosure. Right away Sammie remembered what Eli had said that day at the frolic about calves being a risky business. When the two boys were well away from Eli,

Sammie said, "It looks to me like turkeys are more risky than calves."

"Why?" Oley asked.

"Cause your dad once said calves are risky business. Now your turkeys are dying, too." Sammie said.

Oley stared at Sammie! Sammie could see him turn red with anger! Before he knew what had happened, Oley had struck him. Sammie knew better than to strike back, but by now he was angry, too. In a moment, both of them were hitting as fast as they could.

"Oley! Sammie!" Eli yelled, "Quit it this minute!"

Mom had seen it too and was coming toward them.

"For shame, Sammie!" she exclaimed.

Mom and Eli made the boys apologize and promise to behave, then they left them alone. Both boys said a short "sorry," but for the rest of the day they didn't play with each other.

Sammie followed Eli Mullet around in his work. He watched as he put brightly colored marbles in the feed to attract the baby turkeys' attention. Most of the little birds were eating now, and the worst of the problem was over.

That evening on the way home Mom asked Sammie, "Just what could have caused you and Oley to fight like that?"

"He hit me first," Sammie quickly answered.

"That's not what I mean," Mom said. "What was it that got you in the quarrel in the first place."

Sammie didn't want to tell. He knew that it all started from what he had said about turkeys being as risky as calves or worse. He knew Mom would not like it and maybe she would tell Dad. Then there would be trouble, real trouble.

But there was no choice. Mom kept asking questions until the whole story was out.

"I am very disappointed in you, Sammie," Mom said sadly. "You made it sound like you were glad that they were having bad luck."

Sammie didn't answer. Secretly he had thought it served Eli right after what he had said about the calves.

"It is wrong to rejoice over other people's misfortunes," Mom explained further, "and suppose Oley tells his dad what you said. He may think our whole family feels that way. I can honestly say I feel sorry about their bad luck, and I'm sure Dad will feel that way, too. You should be ashamed of yourself."

Now Sammie began thinking. What had he done? He hadn't dreamed that one little remark could grow into such a big thing! For the first time he began feeling truly sorry about it. Sammie dreaded going to church at Eli Mullets' on Sunday. Suppose Eli would be angry with him. Worse yet, suppose Eli would be angry with Dad and Mom and it would all be his fault.

Sunday morning Sammie wished he could stay home, but he knew that was out of the question. One had to be pretty sick to stay home from church, and Sammie couldn't find anything wrong with himself anywhere.

So on Sunday morning, Sammie held his breath as Eli came walking toward them. He watched his every move and expected any moment to hear what Eli thought of them.

But Eli cracked his usual smile and shook Dad's hand. Then he reached down and shook first Sammie's and then Dannie's hand. Sammie was relieved. That day Sammie and Oley played with each other as if nothing had happened. Sammie was happy that things were again back to normal, but he never did forget the lesson he had learned. It had been a deep lesson for him. He would have to be more careful what he said in the future.

The next day was Monday, the day that Mom always did her laundry. Early in the morning she built a fire under the kettle in the wash house to heat water. When it was hot, she poured it into the gray, square-tub washing machine. Then, with her foot, she pushed the pedal over and over until the gas engine, which operated the agitator, started.

Sammie helped her and Lydia stayed with Baby David in the house. When a load of wash was finished, Mom set the basket full of wet laundry on the little red wagon, and Sammie pulled it outside to the clotheslines. There he waited until she had the things all hung up.

Suddenly Dad came running around the corner of the chicken house.

"Bees are swarming!" he called going into the shed. He came back out carrying two pieces of metal. He ran past the beehives and along the edge of the cornfield. Then he began banging the two pieces of metal.

Sammie started to follow, but Mom said, "You had better stay back, Sammie."

So he stood at the edge of the yard and watched.

On and on Dad pounded and banged the metal pieces together. He was walking along the fence row, and then he stopped. But he kept on banging for a little while. When he stopped banging, Mom said, "Okay, Sammie, now you may run and take a look at the swarm if you like."

So he ran to see, but he didn't go too close. The swarm had settled on a low branch in the fence row. The bees all clung together and formed a clump the size of a basketball. The whole thing was alive with bees flying, crawling and buzzing around that ball.

Dad went quickly back to the shop and brought back a new hive body. He set it under the swarm, working steadily and slowly. He wasn't afraid to work around swarming bees. He had told Sammie that swarming bees don't sting, but Sammie didn't believe it because once, during a swarm, he had received a sting right smack on the eye.

But Dad kept on working and the bees didn't bother him. He put a white cloth around the hive to catch any bees that missed the mark. When all was ready, he reached out and took a firm hold on the branch. He gave it one hefty shake and the whole golden brown clump fell to the open hive body below. Now bees were flying all around Dad and he slowly backed away.

At noon Dad told the children about bees.

"If I hadn't been able to stop them, they would have gone to live in some tree in the woods and we'd have lost them. Bees follow their queen by sound. If you make enough noise, they can't hear her and in the confusion settle down on something. That is what these did. This evening after dark I will go back, close up the hive, and carry it up beside the other two. Then they will begin making honey in the new hive."

Now they would have three hives to gather honey from instead of two. They all loved good, sweet honey on Mom's homemade bread, and there should be plenty to use in her baking recipes, too. They were all happy about the good fortune, and Dad said this was a good, strong swarm, too.

"There is an old saying," Dad said. "A swarm of bees in May is worth a load of hay; A swarm if bees in June is worth a silver spoon; A swarm of bees in July is not worth a fly."

So Sammie knew that this swarm was a good one, because it was only a little past the middle of June.

Chapter 18

The Mysterious Stranger

Now that it was summertime, the little brown calves were taken from their pen and tied outside. East of the barn was a patch of grass that didn't belong to any of the fields, nor was it part of the house yard. It was here that Dad drove a stake into the ground for each calf. Sammie took the calves out and tied each to its stake with a long rope, so that it could munch on the grass inside its own little circle.

It was also Sammie's job to carry feed and water to them. He filled buckets of fresh water at the pump and set them where the calves could reach them. From the feed room in the barn, he carried ground corn and poured the right amount into each of the feed boxes which Dad had made for that purpose.

One day Sammie forgot. He was so busy following Dad around and playing with Lydia and Dannie that he never gave his duties a thought, and, by supper time, the calves still hadn't been fed.

"Sammie, did you feed those calves?" Dad asked.

"No, Dad, I forgot," Sammie answered.

"Forgot?" Dad chided, "Those calves need to be fed before you go to bed."

Just then Sport began barking. He barked like someone was coming, so Dad got up and went to the window. "I can't see anything," he said coming back to the table. Sport quit barking, and they thought no more about it.

After supper Sammie knew that he would have to feed the calves, but the sun had gone down and it would soon be dark. He wished he didn't have to do it alone.

"May Lydia go with me," he asked.

"No, Sammie, go by yourself. Lydia is helping Mom with the dishes. That way you may remember to do your work on time," Dad answered.

So there was no way out. He had to feed the calves, and he had to do it alone. Sammie hurried out and quickly filled the water buckets, and then went after the feed. As he came out of the barn with a pail of ground corn, he thought he saw someone going around the corner of the chicken house, but when he looked closer, he could see no one.

"Dad, were you out by the chicken house a little bit ago?" Sammie asked when he returned to the house.

Dad looked up from his paper, "Do you mean while you were outside?"

"Yes, I thought I saw someone go around the corner of the chicken house, but when I looked closer no one was there," Sammie explained.

"You must have imagined it, because no one was out of the house except you," Dad answered.

Sammie was almost sure he hadn't imagined it. But if Dad said so, then maybe he had.

Just then a knock sounded on the door. Dad and Mom looked at each other and they both looked at Sammie. Dad got slowly to his feet and opened the door. They were quiet as a mouse and listening hard, but they still couldn't hear what the person on the outside said. Then Sammie heard Dad say, "I'll see."

He closed the door and came back.

"There's a tramp at the door. He wants something to eat and a place to sleep," Dad said quietly.

Mom said nothing. Her lips were pressed tightly together and the lines on her face were taut.

Dad thought a moment, then he said, "I guess we can't turn a hungry person away."

Still Mom said nothing, but she nodded slightly. She closed her eyes as Dad went back to the door.

Sammie had often heard Dad talk about tramps. Many times while Dad was growing up, shabbily dressed men would come to the door and ask for food and shelter. They were people without homes who walked around the country living "wherever they took off their hat," as Dad put it.

But this fellow didn't meet the description of those tramps. He was reasonably well dressed and he carried a neat-looking suitcase.

Mom hurried to the kitchen and warmed up supper leftovers. The man sat down and hungrily ate what was set before him. Dad sat and visited with him.

The children peered at the tramp curiously. Baby David, who could walk by now, toddled out and took a good look. Then he hurried back to the safety of Mom's skirts.

The stranger told Dad that his name was Paul Case. He had been out west working, but now was out of work and had no money. He was walking and catching rides to his home and family in the east, and was very happy to find kind people like them along the way.

When he finished eating, he helped Dad carry the rollaway bed into the wash house. Mom brought clean bedding and they left the tramp to settle down for the night.

After Dad and Mom had gone to bed and Sammie and Lydia were settled in their beds upstairs, Sammie lay thinking. He didn't like having that tramp in the house. It put a tenseness in the air that was uncomfortable. Suddenly he heard Lydia tip-toeing down the stairs. He quickly got out of bed and followed her into Mom and Dad's bedroom.

"Mom, I don't like that tramp," Lydia said when they were in their parents bedroom.

"Now, now, Lydia," Mom said gently, "We should love everybody."

"But I don't like it when he is in our house," Lydia insisted.

"Yes, I know, but go back to bed and sleep, now," Mom said.

"I don't want to sleep upstairs," Sammie said then.

Mom got up and helped Sammie and Lydia bed down on the living room lounge, with Sammie sleeping at one end and Lydia at the other. Now they felt much safer. The tramp was still in the house, but Dad and Mom were just inside the bedroom door.

The next morning Mom got the children out of bed and they all went to the barn for chores.

"I suppose you did see someone last night. His tracks are by the chicken house," Dad said to Sammie.

Sammie had figured that out the minute the stranger had come to the door the night before.

"For some reason," Dad went on, "he didn't come right to the house. What I can't figure out, is why Sport didn't keep on barking. You know how he usually carries on when strangers come."

Mom nodded, "I wonder who he is and where he comes from."

"Well, you heard what he said last night, didn't you?" Dad reminded.

"Yes, I know, but ----," she stopped.

"But what?" Dad asked.

"Well," Mom said, "it simply gives me the creeps!"

"Oh, I don't know. He seemed like an honest man." Dad replied, "I can't say I doubt what he said."

When they finished chores, they returned to the house and Mom made breakfast. Their guest was up and ready to go, and ate with them.

After breakfast the stranger thanked Dad for his kindness, nodded his head politely to Mom, picked up his suitcase and went out the door. The whole family watched through the window as he walked toward the road.

Sport stood in the driveway wagging his tail. Why did he act so friendly toward a stranger? Then they saw why. The man reached into his pocket and took out a bit of food. Sport ate it and watched eagerly for more.

"So that is how he did it," Dad laughed. "He is pretty good at making friends with dogs."

They watched as he went on down the road. Sport sat on his haunches at the edge of the driveway and watched, too. After the man passed the Neare farm, a car stopped and picked him up. Then he was gone.

"Well," Mom said with relief, "I hope we don't have anything like that very often."

"I suppose we're just not used to it. Years ago we would have thought nothing of it. Tramps were a common thing." Dad said.

"Maybe we shouldn't say too much about it, for it could be that God sends such a thing to test us," Mom said.

"Possibly," Dad answered. "Anyway, I wouldn't feel right about sending a hungry person away, and I hope he gets back to his family."

"Well, let's quit talking about it," Mom concluded and went back to her work in the kitchen.

A few minutes later Sammie heard excitement out in the yard. He looked outside and saw that Harold Neare had come over and was talking to Dad. Later Dad told them what he had said.

Harold had seen the strange man leaving their farm, and thought that maybe the tramp could be running from the law. He asked Dad lots of questions, but Dad really didn't know much.

"Harold thinks we had a criminal in the house last night," Dad said after he left. "A man guilty of a ---," Dad stopped because Mom shook her head looking at the children sitting there with wide eyes. It was scary, but Sammie wanted very much to hear what Dad was going to say. However, he said no more.

"Anyway," Dad continued, "it does look suspicious, but Harold could be wrong. He is a detective and always has an eye open for trouble."

A few days later Dad came home from town with a paper. It said a hitchhiker had been picked up on the other side of the next town by the sheriff. The man turned out to be wanted by the law.

"It sounds like it may have been our tramp," Dad said.

"What did you say the name was?" Mom asked.

"Here it is," Dad said showing it to her, "Franklin D. Wells."

So now they wondered. Who was who? Was the tramp actually Paul Case as he had said, and was he actually out of work and going back to his family in the east, or had he lied?

"They could easily have been two different people," Dad said. "But it is hard to tell. We will probably never know."

That afternoon Harold came again to talk with Dad. He was sure that the man caught beyond the next town was the tramp who had spent the night in their very house!

"You are probably right," Dad answered.

"Crooks are good at putting up a false front," Harold explained, "In my day I have seen many of them. They are slippery as eels."

Dad and Mom talked about it again at supper time.

"That settles it, I guess," Dad said.

"Well, at least he wasn't unkind to us," Mom concluded.

"No," Dad agreed, "We can be thankful for that."

The next day Mom was cleaning the wash-house. Suddenly Sammie saw her hurrying toward the barn looking for Dad. "Look what I found," she said. In her hand was a well-worn billfold, which she handed to him.

Dad opened it and a smile spread across his face. "P E C," he read, pointing to the worn initials which were carved into the leather. "I guess that fits Paul Case better than Franklin Wells. I guess I never really did believe he was a criminal.

The billfold didn't hold much money, but there was an address in it which matched what the man had told them. The next day Dad wrapped the billfold and sent it to that address.

The whole family was happy. Hopefully Paul Case would soon be with his family in the east, and he'd have his billfold back as well.

Sammie was happy that the man had not turned out to be a criminal. But just the same, it had been a scare. One thing was certain, and he had learned one lesson well. He made sure the calves were fed well before evening after that!

Chapter 19

Blackberries and Willow Whistles

The first of July came, and blackberries were ripening. In the lowlands near the river stood acres and acres of prickly brambles, all loaded with the large, juicy fruits. Dad hitched Queen to the buggy, and the whole family went berry picking.

They picked berries for a couple of hours, and then stopped for lunch. Mom unpacked the picnic she had brought, and she and Baby David and Dannie sat on the buggy to eat. Dad, Sammie and Lydia ate sitting on the cool grass. They had sandwiches of home-cured ham between slices of home-made bread and, for dessert, they each had a half-moon pie. It all got washed down with a glass of rich, chocolate milk.

After lunch Mom tried to put Dannie and Baby David to sleep, but Sammie and Lydia were playing and making too much noise.

"Come, children," Dad finally said, "Let's go for a walk."

They took hold of Dad's hands and walked with him down to the river.

"Ei, look down there!" Dad said, pointing.

A mother mallard duck, followed by a row of babies, was swimming upstream pretty as a picture.

"One, two, three, four, five, six, seven!" Sammie said as he proudly counted the babies.

"See there!" Lydia exclaimed, pointing further back. Two more baby ducks were hurrying to catch up with the others. Little waves spread out behind them and disappeared in the current.

Along the banks stood lots of box elder and plum bushes and willow trees. Dad stopped by a young willow and said, "When I was a boy, we used to make willow whistles. Would you like one?"

"Yes! Yes!" they both chimed together.

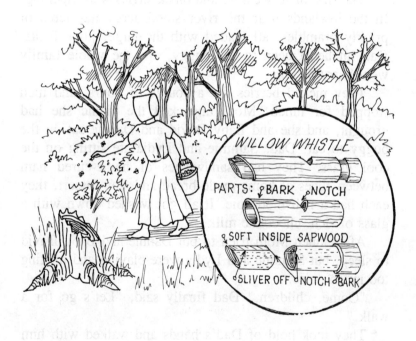

Dad took out his pocket knife and went to work. He cut off a twelve-inch long piece of tender, new growth the size of his little finger, and trimmed the small end off at an angle. Two inches back from the angle cut, he carved out a notch. Going back two more inches, he made a cut all the way around through the tender, green bark. Then, holding the willow stick firmly against his knee, he thoroughly hammered the bark with the handle of his knife all the way around the twig.

He then laid his knife down and, holding the unpounded end of the willow stick with his left hand and the section he had pounded with his right, he carefully twisted. The bark in the pounded area came loose and slid off smoothly all in one piece, leaving the clean, bare wood.

"Here," he said to Sammie, "hold this."

Sammie held the piece of bark and watched as Dad cut a thin slice of wood from the top of the bare stick, between the end and the notch. Then he cut the stick through, right in the middle of the notch. He took the bark cylinder from Sammie and inserted the short piece of bare wood back into it, so it again fit perfectly from the notch to the tapered end, leaving a narrow opening along the top.

Dad then cut off the excess part of the stick, leaving only a finger-width of bark behind the bare wood, inserted that piece back into its place inside the bark cylinder, and the whistle was done.

Dad blew in at the tapered end and out came a clear, pleasant sound. He slid the stick end out a bit and blew again, creating a different tone. He then handed the whistle to Sammie and said to Lydia, "Do you want one, too?"

"Yes," she said eagerly.

While Sammie tried out his whistle, Lydia watched closely while Dad made another. This one was smaller than Sammie's and had a higher pitch. Between the two of them, they could produce many different sounds as they slid the stick ends back and forth. The children kept whistling all the way back to the buggy, but as they got close, Dad hushed them.

"Now put the whistles away," he said. "We don't want to wake the little ones."

The children put the whistles into their pockets, grabbed their little berry buckets, and went back to picking berries.

Dad noticed that Sammie and Lydia's little pails didn't fill up very fast, and teased them, saying, "You two are canning your berries right away. That is why your pails don't fill up." But Sammie knew Dad didn't really mind. In the morning he had told them they could eat as many as they wished while they picked.

"Such faces!" Mom exclaimed when they came back to the buggy to go home. She took out her handkerchief and tried to wipe off the blackberry stains. She rubbed until it hurt, but it did no good. The stains would not come off!

"Well, I guess it can't be helped," she finally said.

The blackberry stains didn't bother the children nearly as much as the mosquito bites on their necks and arms. They squirmed and scratched, but it did no good. They scratched until the bites bled and Mom told them to quit.

In spite of the stains and the mosquito bites, they were all happy. Sammie was glad they had so many blackberries, because now they could have cold blackberry soup and Mom could bake blackberry pies and make blackberry jelly to spread on slices of good home-made bread.

Sammie and Lydia were also happy because they each had a willow whistle in their pocket. When they got home, they took them out again and tried to blow them, but no sound came out. They were very disappointed. When Dad saw that they were having problems, he said, "Put them in water. When the whistles dry out, they don't work."

After the whistles were soaked, they worked perfectly again.

Chapter 20

Threshing Time

The weather was warm and dry. The winds blew across the flat lands, causing the grain fields to wave back and forth like a golden sea which never comes to a complete rest.

All summer long the barley had grown. Finally it had headed out and changed from a deep green to a pale green and at last to a golden brown.

Dad hitched Mollie, Dollie and Tim to the binder and drove around the field cutting the grain. It was exciting to see, and the children loved to watch. The grain stalks were snipped off by the sickle, pushed neatly by a constantly revolving reel onto the platform web and carried swiftly to the elevator webs right under Dad's feet.

At the upper end of the elevator webs, the grain stalks came flowing out and slid down the slanted floor to lodge against the tripping lever. Little steel arms came up through the slanted floor and pushed and shook the barley stalks until enough had been gathered to make a sheave.

Then all in one quick motion, the needle came up, the knot was tied, and a neat bundle of ripe barley was kicked out onto the carrier underneath the binder. It happened so fast that Sammie could never quite see everything that happened in that instant. No sooner had one been kicked out than another was being tied.

As the children stood watching, Sammie was thinking. Dad and Mom had told them a story about a little boy who

went through the binder. He was playing in the field where his father was cutting grain. Somehow, he got into the path of the binder, and was pushed onto the platform by the reel. The little boy came out tied neatly into a bundle, but wasn't hurt, except for a few bruises. It was hard to imagine a person going through that machine without getting hurt!

All day long Dad kept on cutting barley. The horses had to walk swiftly to keep the binder running smoothly. Mollie and Dollie could be counted on to keep a steady pace, but Tim was not as dependable. If Tim slowed down, Dad called, "Giddap, Tim!" and touched his rump with the long bamboo stick which rested in the socket near the levers.

Dad had many things to keep track of as he drove along. He had to guide the horses so that Mollie stayed next to the uncut barley. He had four levers in front of him to keep everything on the binder set just right. His left foot controlled a pedal that dropped and raised the bundle carrier. When Dad had seven bundles of barley on the carrier, he looked out of the corner of his eye to line up with the pile of bundles he had dropped on the last round, then raised his foot and the carrier dropped to the ground. The tines slid out from under the bundles, leaving the pile sitting there. Then quickly, before another sheave was kicked out, he had to push the pedal down to bring the carrier back up into place. So on it went. The rows of barley bundles kept getting longer and longer until the whole field was cut.

That evening, Sammie helped Dad build the barley shocks. They placed three sheaves in a row, then two on each side. Next Dad took a sheaf, bent down the heads, and placed it on top for a roof.

The bearded barley Dad had planted was very prickly, and in no time at all Sammie's arms, neck and face were scratched and red. He looked at Dad and saw that, even though it was warm, Dad was wearing long sleeves to protect his arms from being scratched. As the barley heads didn't reach his neck, he didn't need any protection there.

After the barley was done, Dad and Sammie cut the oats. Oats didn't cause any itchiness, so Sammie liked them better.

Soon the grain was all cut. Row after row of beautiful shocks stood in the fields waiting to be threshed. Every shock had a little roof made of a bundle of grain which protected the sheaves from summer rains. For two weeks the grain dried under the hot July sun, and then it was time to do the threshing.

Ezra Yoder was the threshing boss for the community. Early one morning he arrived, riding on top of the huge threshing machine, which was being drawn by two large black horses.

Behind him came one of his sons driving another team. They were pulling a strange looking rig. The wheels and the frame looked just like a wagon, but mounted crosswise on the beams was a large green engine. On one end of the engine was a wide pulley. The other end looked like the front of a tractor. Dad called it the "power unit".

Ezra and his son had come early to set up the machine before the other neighbors arrived. The threshing couldn't begin until the dew was gone from the fields.

The men set up next to the granary. They lined the power unit up with the threshing machine, attached the forty-foot long flat drive belt to the pulleys, and then adjusted the blower pipe and the grain chute. Grease gun in hand, Ezra walked, crawled and climbed to every spot on the thresher and pumped grease into all the fittings.

When Uncle Andy drove up to the machine with the first wagon-load of bundles, everything was ready to go. Ezra started up the power unit and the long black belt began moving. Faster, faster, and faster it went until the machine was fairly humming.

As Sammie watched, Uncle Andy began throwing in bundles. They landed on a conveyer belt which took them into the machine. Two devices which looked like arms pounded the sheaves and cut the twines. Belts and pulleys went spinning around and around and shakers moved back and forth. Sammie loved to watch the bundles disappear into the thresher and listen to its humming as it separated the grain from the straw and chaff. Wagon after wagon brought bundles from the fields and the men pitched them in. When the barley was done, they started on the oats.

All day long the clean threshed and winnowed grain flowed steadily into the bin. The straw was blown out the large pipe at the rear and landed on a wood frame in the barnyard, creating a straw stack with a cozy room under it where the young stock would have a warm place to sleep next winter.

Mom was very busy in the house, and Sammie had to quit watching to carry potatoes from the root cellar. It took a lot of food to feed the threshers, so Aunt Lena had come to help.

At noon Ezra shut down the threshing machine and the men paused long enough to wash up in the yard and to eat Mom's good dinner. As soon as they were done, they came out chewing on their toothpicks. Ezra started up the engine and in a few minutes they were back to work. Oat dust flew from the machine and drifted all over the barnyard and the driveway and the lawn and onto the chicken house roofs.

It was a hot day. In the afternoon Sammie and Lydia filled a jug with cold water, put it and some glasses on the little red wagon, and pulled it around giving drinks to the threshers. The men stopped only long enough to wipe the sweat from their foreheads and take a cool drink, and then went right back to work.

Just before chore time, Mom sent the children out with sandwiches and chocolate milk. Again Ezra shut everything down, and all was quiet while the men ate sandwiches and washed them down with the cold, sweet chocolate milk.

Everyone went back to threshing except Dad, who had to do his chores. All through chores the machine hummed steadily on.

"Ezra is trying to get this job done before dark," Dad explained.

It was sundown when the last load of bundles came from the field. Already some of the wagons were heading home. The last wagons to unload had to hurry because there were no lights on them, and it would soon be dark.

Dad helped Ezra clean up around the threshing machine. With scoop shovels they threw the last oats onto the conveyer, and then Ezra walked to the power unit, cut the throttle, pulled a lever, and everything came to a stop. A great stillness came over the little farm, and the dust finally settled. The last wagon was heading south on the gravel road. The high-pitched sound of its steel wheels on the road floated back to the farm until it was far away.

Ezra didn't have a wagon or a buggy there, and, as it would soon be dark, he couldn't take the threshing machine home.

"That's no problem," Dad said, "You can leave your teams here and borrow a horse and buggy from us."

So they hitched Queen up to the buggy and Dad got out the lanterns. He lit them and hung one on each side of the buggy. On the front side of each lantern, the light shone out through clear glass. On the back side was a red lens which the yellow flame shone through also, and that served as a tail light. Sammie watched the lanterns as Ezra drove away.

The next morning Ezra came early, hitched his black team to the threshing machine, climbed on top, and drove away. Dad hitched Ezra's other team to the power unit and followed. Threshing on the little farm was over, and for days after that, Dad went from farm to farm with the crew to help all the neighbors who had helped him.

Every night Dad came home very late and very tired. He didn't tell stories or sit reading, because it was soon bedtime, and the next morning he would have to leave again early. So it was a welcome change when Sunday came, and they all dressed up and went to church.

That afternoon Aunt Lena invited the family to come by later for supper. The children were happy about that. They'd have to go home and do chores, but then back to Uncle Andys' they would go. When Uncle Andy and Dad were hitching up, Sammie ran and asked, "Dad, may I ride home with Uncle Andys?"

Dad looked at him and thought for a moment, "Oh, I guess you may. If you behave yourself, that is."

"I will," Sammie said quickly.

He and cousin Jonas whooped and ran with all their might to Uncle Andy's carriage. He had two sleek black horses hitched to the double-seated buggy. Aunt Lena and the girls sat on the back seat and Jonas and Sammie sat in front.

It was very exciting for Sammie to ride in such a fast-moving buggy! Uncle Andy drove with both hands. The horses and the double tree and the neck yoke and the harness moved in perfect rhythm. The flying hooves seemed to barely touch the ground as the horses trotted swiftly down the road. The wind blew into their faces and the boys had to hold their hats.

Jonas pushed his father and said, "Dad, make them go really fast!"

But Uncle Andy paid no attention to him. Sammie didn't care. This was the fastest ride he had ever had behind horses.

"Don't you wish you had fast horses, too?" Jonas asked.

Sammie didn't say anything.

"I'm glad we don't have a slow, ploddy horse like Queen," Jonas went on.

"Jonas," Uncle Andy said sternly looking sideways at him.

So Jonas said no more.

Sammie sat thinking. He liked Queen, but right now it bothered him that she wasn't fast. He had been enjoying the fast ride, but now it was all spoiled, and he wished he had gone home with Dad and Mom.

That night, after a nice visit and a good supper, Dad and Mom and Sammie and Lydia and Dannie and Baby David were all on the buggy going home. Queen was trotting along at her usual speed and Sammie sat thinking.

"Dad," he finally said, "Jonas said Queen is slow and ploddy."

Dad laughed a little, then he said, "What did you say then?"

"I didn't say anything," Sammie answered.

"Well, I'm glad that you didn't get into another quarrel," Dad answered. "What Jonas said 'will go home with him.' You needn't worry too much about that. Queen is a safe horse, and she takes us where we want to go. I don't think we should feel ashamed of her."

Now Sammie was glad that he hadn't said anything. Listening to Dad made him feel much better, but he went on thinking. He listened contently to the clop-clop of Queen's feet on the hard road surface.

Lydia was leaning against him, fast asleep. Sammie was tired too, but all the way home, he watched the glow of the lantern. Puffs of wind caused the yellow flame to flicker and cast a dancing light on his face. Shadows stretched away from the spokes of the wheels and moved with the buggy through the dark night. No one talked because it had been a busy week and they were all tired. Finally Sammie saw the dim outline of their own buildings. They were all glad to be home.

Chapter 21

A Safe Horse

The next morning at milking time, the children's favorite cow, Bessie, didn't come to the barn. Afterwards, Dad went looking and found her stretched out and bloated to death. Her one hind leg was caught in the fence. Later, Dad explained to the children what had probably happened.

"By the looks of it, she got caught in the fence, then either lay or fell down. That wouldn't have hurt her, except she happened to be lying tilted back and with her head down hill. A cow in that position will fill up with gases and if the gases aren't released soon enough, it will kill her," Dad explained.

The children looked sorrowfully at Bessie, but they knew there was nothing they could do to bring her back.

Mom had a list of things she needed from town. The sugar and the flour bins were almost empty, the baking powder was all gone, and she needed supplies so she could finish the summer canning. Also, it was already the middle of August, and soon the children would need shoes again.

"Shoes will have to wait, yet," Dad said.

Their luck that year had been mostly bad, and there wasn't much money. First the calves had been sick. Then Queen had had a colt which died, and Sammie had heard Dad tell Mom that the milk price on the Cleveland market had fallen to half of what it had been before. Now Bessie was dead, plus there was something wrong with the sows.

They didn't have many baby pigs, and the ones they did have were weak and some had already died.

"If I could just get jar lids and sugar, I could go on with the canning," Mom said then.

"Okay," Dad answered, "I will put new shoes on Queen, then you can go to town this afternoon."

Dad brought Queen out of the barn and tied her by the shed, got his horse-shoeing tools from the shop, and fastened his leather apron around his waist. He was now ready to work.

Dad had shod horses for other people before he married, and still liked to do it. And the children loved to watch him.

Dad petted Queen to reassure her, and then moved his hand down her right front leg. With his forefinger and thumb, he put a little pressure on the muscle just above the fetlock and she lifted her foot for him.

Holding Queen's foot firmly between his legs, and whistling as he worked, Dad took his hoof knife and cut out some of the sole. Next he used a sharp pincer to clip off the hoof around the outside. Then, drawing his rasp back and forth along the bottom of the hoof, he leveled the foot. He then leaned back, pushing the foot down with the end of the rasp, and sighted across the hoof to check if it was level yet. He filed some more and sighted again.

When the hoof looked just right, Dad laid an iron shoe on it and nailed it on. Sometimes the nail bent and wouldn't go in. Then Dad would pull it out, lay it on the shoe, tap it with the hammer until it was straight, and try again, pounding until it came out of the side of Queen's hoof. Then, with the claw of his hammer, he would bend it over and tap it down flat. Later he would clip the end off with the pincer.

"Doesn't it hurt her?" Lydia asked. "It would hurt me if you'd nail a shoe to my foot."

Dad laughed. Queen stood there sleepily, hardly paying attention to what was happening. "A hoof is a little like your fingernails," Dad explained. "It doesn't hurt a horse if I put the nails in the right place."

When Dad shoed horses, he often recited a poem which he had learned when he was a boy going to school. Sammie loved to hear it, so he asked Dad to say it once more.

> *Under the spreading chestnut tree*
> *The village smithy stands;*
> *The smith a mighty man is he*
> *With large, sinewy hands. . . . .[1]*

It was a long poem, but Dad knew it clear through. Sammie looked at Dad's large hands. It was easy to imagine how the village smithy looked.

When Dad had finished shoeing Queen, she was sharp shod and ready to go.

That afternoon Dad hitched Queen to the buggy, and Mom drove to town. She took Lydia and Dannie and Little David along, but Sammie stayed home. Instead of going down the highway as she usually did, she went south on the gravel road, because she was going to leave the children at the Grabers until she came back.

Sammie began playing with the little red wagon, but with Lydia and Dannie gone, playing was not much fun.

---

[1] *The Village Blacksmith* by Henry W. Longfellow

When he saw Dad going toward the pig pen with a gallon jug, he left the wagon and followed.

"What's in the jug?" Sammie asked.

"Disinfectant," Dad answered. "I think there may be something in these mud puddles that causes the pigs to get sick."

Sammie watched as he poured disinfectant into every puddle.

He was thinking. "Disinfectant." He said the word over and over. It sounded big and strange and important.

"Look at this!" Dad said pointing at a puddle. Where he had poured the disinfectant, the mud slowly churned.

"What is it?" Sammie asked.

"I don't know," Dad answered, "It could be bacteria that causes it to move like that."

"Bacteria." Now he had another big word to say. He had learned two big words in one day.

Just then a car drove in. A gray-haired man got out and walked towards them.

"Say Mister," he said to Dad, "are you the one that drives a white buggy mare?"

"Yes, why?" Dad asked.

"Well, I just came from town and I found her walking this way without a driver," he said.

"Huh," Dad said, "I wonder what happened?"

"I have no idea," the man went on, "but she was walking along like she knew what she was doing. She was on the right side of the road and everything."

"Where is she now?" Dad asked.

"Do you know where Melvin James lives?" the man asked.

Dad nodded.

"Well, I tied her to a fence post just this side of the James farm."

Again Dad nodded, "Thank you! I'm glad for your help!"

He turned and walked away. They watched as he got in his car and drove off. Dad stood thinking, and then he said, "Come Sammie."

They walked down the road to Harold's place. Dad took big steps and Sammie had to run to keep up. Harold listened as Dad told him what the problem was.

"Let's go right away," Harold said, jumping in his pickup truck.

Dad and Sammie got in on the other side, and they drove down the highway toward town. Halfway to town they met Mom with Queen and the buggy, driving along like normal. They waved and Mom waved back.

"Everything seems under control," Harold said. He slowed down the pickup and turned around.

They slowly passed the buggy, looking back to see if Mom needed help, but Mom waved them on.

"What do I owe you?" Dad asked as Harold dropped them off.

"Not a thing. I'm just glad everything turned out okay," Harold answered.

"Well, I'm much obliged to you," Dad answered.

When Mom came home, she told them what had happened. She had dropped off the children at the Grabers' and gone on to town.

"When I wanted to tie Queen behind the grocery store, there was no rope on the buggy," she said.

"What?" Dad asked, looking at the children, "Where did that rope get to?"

Sammie looked at Lydia and Lydia looked at Sammie and Dannie. All three knew what had happened. They told Dad that the day before they had been playing on the buggy and had used the rope to tie up their make-believe horse. They just forgot to put it back.

"Well, anyway," Mom continued, "I just tied her with the hitching strap. But when I came back out of the store she was gone. I could hardly believe it, because I wasn't in there very long. I looked up and down the streets, but she was nowhere in sight."

"Hadn't anyone else seen her leave?" Dad asked.

"I don't know. Nobody I saw seemed to know anything about it," Mom sighed a little and went on. "I didn't know what to do. Finally I decided to go on over to the mill store since you had wanted calf feed anyway. I told the owner my problem. He immediately said he'd go after her. He put the calf feed on the truck and we picked up my groceries. Then we headed out of town toward home. After a while I thought maybe we had gone the wrong way."

"Why so?" Dad asked.

"Because I couldn't believe she had gone that far," Mom answered.

"Sometimes time goes faster than we think," Dad said.

"Finally we came to her tied to a post by the side of the road, so someone must have caught her," Mom said.

"That is how we found out about it," Dad explained. "The man who caught her stopped in here and told us. I don't even know who he was. In the excitement I forgot to ask."

"Well, I was shaking all over," Mom shuddered a little. "I had imagined all sorts of things. One thing is sure. I'm glad we have a safe buggy horse!"

"She probably would have come all the way home if no one had stopped her," Dad said.

"The man from the mill loaded my things into the buggy and held on to Queen's bridle until I was ready to start out. I was ever so grateful! I offered to pay him for his trouble, but he just waved it aside. He said he was glad to see everything turn out okay," Mom said.

"So was I," Dad said, "I didn't know what to think when that guy told us he had found Queen without a driver."

"Well, I'm glad it is over. It could have been a lot worse!" Mom said gratefully.

"Well, children," Dad said, "I think you had better put that rope back on the buggy. This should teach you a lesson. Bad things can easily happen out of such carelessness. I don't mind if you play with that rope, but remember to put it back where it belongs."

Right away they ran out and put the rope back on the buggy. They didn't want Queen to get loose in town again.

But Sammie was proud of her. From now on when Cousin Jonas bragged about his father's horses, Sammie would have something good to say about Queen, too!

Chapter 22

Barn Fire!

It was late summer, and the weather was hot and sultry. The cows were lazy in the warm weather and preferred to lie in the shade along the woods. They wouldn't come to the barn on their own at milking time, so it became Sammie's job to fetch them.

Late each afternoon Sammie would travel along the dusty cowpath to get the cows. He usually walked with his head down looking at the prints in the dust. He could see where birds had hopped, and closer to the woods, he sometimes found tracks of squirrels and raccoons.

One evening Sammie, who had gotten started later than usual and was in a hurry, was trotting along when suddenly a snake slithered across the path just ahead of him, right where his foot was about to land. He tried to avoid the step, but it was too late! His bare foot came down right smack on the snake's back!

Sammie took off running with all his might! A few hundred feet down the path, he stopped and looked back, but the snake was nowhere in sight. He looked at his foot. He couldn't see anything, but the sensation of his bare foot lighting on the back of a snake made goose pimples come out all over his arms. He wondered what the snake had done. It probably increased its own speed as much as Sammie did! Maybe it even had some goose pimples of it's own! Sammie continued on to get the cows, and by the time he got back to the barn with them, the goose pimples were gone.

The next afternoon, the children were playing on the swing under the oak tree. Mom was also outside, hanging the Sunday clothes on the line to get them ready for church the next day.

Suddenly Mom came around the corner of the house sniffing the air. She looked toward the southwest and then ran quickly to the barn.

It took the puzzled children only a moment to discover why Mom had acted so strangely, as their noses picked up the smell of smoke in the air and they saw, from behind the woods to the southwest, a large billow of smoke rising high into the sky. Something big was burning!

Dad came out of the barn carrying a pitchfork. One look and he dropped it and ran toward the road.

"It must be at the Grabers'!" he called over his shoulder.

He crossed the road, climbed the fence, ran across the oat stubble field, rounded the corner of the woods and Sammie couldn't see him anymore.

They could hear the sirens wailing as the fire trucks from town came to fight the fire. Sammie looked again toward the Graber farm. The billow of smoke was larger now, and he could see a red glow above the woods.

Mom harnessed Queen to the buggy, loaded the children in, and headed quickly down the road to the south.

"Oh, I wonder what is burning!" Mom exclaimed over and over.

When they came out from behind the woods, they could see that the Grabers' barn was on fire. The whole thing was engulfed in flames!

They turned the corner and drove down the dirt road. Cars kept passing them, stirring up dust so thick it was

hard to see. The air was dense with smoke also, making breathing difficult. Mom got out her handkerchief and held it over her mouth and nose, and helped each of the children do the same.

The Grabers' driveway and yard were full of cars and trucks and people. Mom drove into a field near the house and tied Queen to a post. She and the other children went to the house to be with Mrs. Graber. Sammie didn't want to go in, so Mom said, "Okay, but stay out of people's way and don't go away from the house."

Now Sammie could hear the crackling of the fire. Parts of the roof had already fallen in, and just then the south wall let loose and fell with a crash. Sparks flew and rose with the smoke.

Sammie saw Dad hurrying around helping the firemen.

The rest of the sides fell in and more sparks flew. The wind fanned the blaze and seemed to almost lift the burning barn off the ground. The firemen sprayed water, which hissed and steamed as it hit the fire. Steam rose and disappeared in the smoke.

The farm looked very strange. It didn't look like the Grabers' home at all. The barn was down to a burning heap. People were all about. Firemen called to each other and hurried around. They kept spraying water, and the fire trucks kept going to the river for more.

Gradually the fire died down. Where the barn had been was an ugly pile of burning feed and smoldering timbers. Thick smoke rose from the pile. Strong smells of burning feed filled the air and almost choked Sammie, it smelled so terrible!

Freeman and Abner were running around and playing like usual. Sammie looked at them and wondered how they could have fun while their dad's barn was burning.

One by one the people left, and finally Dad and Mom and the children got in the buggy and went home.

"It is a good thing the cows and horses were out on pasture," Dad said as they drove down the dusty road toward home.

"Oh yes," Mom agreed, "But Mrs. Graber was almost beside herself. She thinks the fire started from sparks while she was burning trash."

"Well, I don't know. Orin thinks the cause was wet hay," Dad answered.

"Anyway, I tried to comfort her. There were no people hurt. There is so much to be thankful for," Mom said.

Dad kept talking about the fire all the way home. A small calf had perished, but all the rest of the animals were safe.

"I sure feel sorry for them," Dad said. "Their whole years supply of hay and straw and oats was in there. Orin and Allen were very sad about it. I told Orin that I'd be over first thing Monday morning to help clean up."

Other neighbors would come to help clean up the burned mess also. Then they'd cut down trees and saw logs, and, in the end, there would be a great barn raising. It would all take time, but the Grabers would again have a barn.

Sammie sat in front of the buggy thinking. He thought about the barn which had so quickly changed into a pile of ashes. He thought about the poor calf that had perished in the fire. It all seemed very sad. He thought about Freeman and Abner. He thought about what Mom said about being thankful. Some things were hard to understand. How could wet hay start a fire?

That night after chores were done and supper was over, the family was sitting in the living room.

"Dad," Sammie said.

"What do you want, Sammie?" Dad asked turning toward him.

"Dad, how can a fire start from wet hay?" Sammie asked.

"Well, it can. When you put a pile of wet hay in the barn, it will heat up and form gas. Inside the pile the gas can't get away, so it keeps building up and building up until it explodes," Dad explained.

"Do you think our hay could explode, too?" Sammie asked.

"Hardly. I think ours was all good and dry," Dad answered.

Sammie's thoughts went back to haymaking time. The hay had seemed very dry. He was glad about that.

Chapter 23

Sammie Goes To School

The first day of school was only ten days away. Sammie still didn't have new shoes because Dad said they simply couldn't afford them. When Dad talked about all the bad luck, Mom always said, "We still have lots to be thankful for. If the bad luck stays in the barn, we shouldn't complain. We're all healthy and have plenty to eat."

"Yes, I guess you're right," Dad answered.

"The tomatoes look like a good crop. Maybe that will help us get on our feet financially," Mom said hopefully.

"Yes," Dad agreed, "If it wasn't for that, I would start thinking about doing something else."

Sammie was all ears, now. He wondered what Dad meant by "something else".

The tomatoes were beginning to ripen. Mom brought some in and sliced them for dinner. The whole family loved fresh sliced tomatoes except Dad. He liked almost anything Mom put on the table, but not tomatoes, and they enjoyed teasing him about it.

Already before they sat down to eat, Lydia said, "I want the tomato juice."

After the last slice was taken from the plate, there was usually some juice left in the bottom, which they sprinkled salt on and drank from the plate. Drinking this juice was very important to the children, and they often quarreled about who was going to get it.

Sammie whined, "I asked for it first!"

"I asked for it before you even came in!" Lydia retorted.

"Now, now, children," Mom chided, "You should take turns. Let Sammie have it today, because he is older. Lydia can have it tomorrow and so on by the age."

So Lydia had to give up, but the next day it was her turn and Sammie wished he had let her have it the day before. They both had to wait for their turn, and wishing for the tomato juice before then did no good.

"I can't figure out what is so great about that salted tomato juice," Dad teased them, "but if all of you like tomatoes so well, I won't eat any away from you."

There were plenty of ripe tomatoes in the field now. Dad went to Harolds' and called the canning factory. The next day they expected to see pickers in the field, but nobody came. A few days later Dad called again. Still no pickers came.

"At least we have plenty of tomatoes to eat and for canning," Mom said looking on the bright side of things.

"That doesn't do me a lot of good," Dad said with a wry smile. "I wonder what the problem is. For some reason they are 'slow as molasses in January.' Tomatoes are rotting in the field."

That afternoon Dad hitched Queen to the buggy and went away. Just before chore time he came driving home again. He had been to the canning factory, and at supper time he told the family what had happened.

"Tomatoes are a heavy crop this year. The cannery is simply swamped with them. I could see that as soon as I got there," Dad said.

"Won't they take any of ours?" Mom asked.

"Well, yes, they say they will. But when I asked for a specific time when they would begin picking, they were reluctant to answer. I finally asked to see the agent who made the contract with us last spring, but they said he wasn't there."

"Of course not," Mom put in.

"But I was bound to get a decent answer before I left," Dad went on, "so I asked to see the person in charge of the place. They just looked at each other and wouldn't tell me where he was."

"Didn't you show them the contract?" Mom asked.

"Well no, but they know well enough how it is. Anyway, I kept on until they did let me talk to the foreman. He gave me more satisfaction. He simply told me that they just have more tomatoes than they can handle. We are not the only grower who is being ignored. They are taking care of their large growers first."

"That's not fair! What about the contract? Doesn't that mean anything?" Mom asked.

"I asked about that, too. What about next year? How can growers trust them from now on? He got a little uncomfortable when I said that. Finally he said we could either hire pickers ourselves or wait a few days and they'd come pick them."

"What did you decide then?" Mom asked.

"I told him I didn't know where to find pickers. He finally agreed to have pickers out here first thing Monday morning, and I left it at that. I suppose we could get them in trouble if we'd press charges in court, but I wouldn't want to do that," Dad said.

"Maybe they know we won't press charges," Mom said.

Dad shrugged, "It is going to be hard to sit around and watch five acres of good tomatoes go to waste when they could just as well be picked. The way they are ripening, a lot of tomatoes can spoil in three days. But, I guess this is the best we can do. And it could be worse. North of here, near Bluffton, a picker was struck by lightning yesterday during that rain we had, and it killed him."

"Yes," Mom agreed, "we'd feel bad if something like that happened in our field."

The next day Sammie was looking for Dad. He found him in the tomato field. When he came closer he saw that Dad was eating a tomato! How Sammie laughed! Dad laughed, too, and said, "I guess we might as well eat some if they are this plentiful!" Dad was being funny, but the problem was real. Tons of tomatoes were rotting in the field.

In two more days the pickers would come, but Sammie would not be home to see them. Monday was going to be Sammie's first day in school, but getting Sammie to school was another problem. The school house was four miles away, which was much too far for a little boy to walk, and Sammie couldn't take a horse and buggy by himself.

Then Dad came home and said the problem was solved. Orin Graber's children, he said, were going to drive to school with horse and buggy. They would pass through Walnut Corners, which was less than a mile to the south, and Sammie could walk there and catch a ride with them.

"That should work pretty good," Dad said.

Sammie knew he should be happy that things were working out, but he had misgivings. To begin with, he'd have to ride to school every day with Freeman, who had always been mean to him. The second thing was that the stretch of gravel road between home and Walnut Corners had some pretty scary spots. He'd have to walk past the woods, which wasn't too bad, but beyond that was an old abandoned farmstead, and that place worried him.

Monday morning came and Mom helped Sammie get ready. She combed his blonde hair down and snugly tied his hat strings under his chin. Patting him on the back, she said, "Be a good boy in school, Sammie," and handed him a paper bag containing a pencil, a ruler and a tablet. He took the bag in one hand and his lunch box in the other and started out.

Sammie crossed the highway and walked down the gravel road. The signs of the coming fall were all around. The goldenrod had already put on its brilliant yellow tops and, along the road, the ragweed was so tall that he couldn't see the oat stubble on the other side.

Sammie walked on. He went past a low spot where cattails grew and continued on through the woods. As he crossed over a small bridge, he came to the part he dreaded. Just ahead on his left was the old abandoned farmstead. Both the house and barn roofs were falling in, and everything was overgrown with weeds and grass and small trees. An old grapevine clung to the side of the house, and an unkempt hedge stood along the road. He couldn't see what all was on the other side of that.

Sammie stopped and looked back the way he had come. Home was hidden behind the woods. He turned forward again and swiftly walked past the old place and on to the corner.

Soon the Graber children came driving down the road in an open, two-seated carriage. Freeman and Abner sat in the front seat and Elsie and Ella, the twin girls, sat in the back. Freeman stopped the horse.

Sammie went between the wheels to climb on the front seat.

Freeman threw back his head and said, "Get in the back!"

Sammie stopped. He wasn't sure he had heard right. Surely he would sit up front with the boys.

"Sit in the back seat!" Freeman repeated.

So Sammie turned and climbed on the back. The girls pulled back the duster and made room for him to sit.

Freeman grabbed the whip from the socket next to the dashboard and cut the horse across the flank. The buggy started with a lurch and they were off for a fast ride to school.

Sammie had had fast rides before when he rode with Uncle Andy, but this was different. Uncle Andy's horses were well-fed and carefully groomed, and showed that they were eager to get going by pulling on the lines. They arched their necks and willingly pulled the buggy where ever Uncle Andy wanted to go. The Grabers, on the other hand, treated their horses poorly, and didn't give them enough feed.

Freeman whipped the horse until it went fast. Its hips stuck out and its ribs showed, but it had to go fast anyway. As soon as it slowed down, it was again urged on with the whip. The horse laid back its ears and showed its displeasure, but went at a good fast trot all the way to school anyway.

Cousin Jonas and Oley Mullet were on the playground when they arrived at school, and Sammie felt better. They talked and played until the teacher came outside and rang a hand-held bell. All the children stopped what they were doing and headed for the schoolhouse, so Sammie did too.

Mrs. Bonnie McPhail was the teacher. She wrote down Sammie's full name, then asked him when his birthday was, and wrote that down, too. He didn't know what year he was born, but he knew he was six years old, going on seven. She thought a little and then wrote something down. At last, she wrote down Dad and Mom's names and was done.

Sammie knew immediately that he liked Mrs. McPhail. She helped him get settled into a seat, smiled when she talked, and patted him on the shoulder before she walked away.

The first day in school was new and exciting. The time went fast and all too soon it was afternoon. When Mrs. McPhail dismissed the children for the day, Sammie had to get on the back seat of the Graber buggy for the ride home. He got a bad feeling in his stomach that wouldn't go away. He was not looking forward, when they dropped him off at the corner, to walking past that old abandoned farmstead again.

Once he was home, he felt better. The tomato pickers were there and were loading a truck with tomatoes. Quickly Sammie changed into his everyday clothes and he and Lydia ran out to watch. They stopped near the tomato pickers and listened to their talk. They were Mexicans, and the children couldn't understand a word they said, but it was fun to listen anyway. With all the excitement, Sammie almost forgot about school. He did his chores and helped Lydia carry wood and dry corn cobs for the kitchen range and everything was as it usually was.

But the next morning came, and he had to go past that old farmstead again on his way to school. While Sammie liked school, he did not like the daily trips to and from school.

How Sammie hated to walk past that old farm. He thought about the many things that could be hiding there. He thought about some of Dad's tramp stories. Maybe a tramp lived there. He thought about the stray dogs which had run around the countryside last year.

One morning it was very windy. Suddenly, as he drew even with the house, he saw something black come up from behind the hedge! It went back out of sight! His heart missed a beat and leaped into his throat and stuck there!

In a moment it appeared again, but again it disappeared so quickly that he could not tell what it was.

Sammie didn't wait for another look. He had seen enough. That thing was black, and it was hard to imagine what could jump that high. He took off running for all he was worth. His lunchbox flew open, scattering food as he went. Without looking up, he turned back, quickly stuffed everything back in the lunchbox, and ran to the corner. Luckily nothing had broken.

When he got to the corner, he looked back to make sure nothing was following him. But he was sure he had seen something. And he was sure it was black. Maybe it was a big black dog, or, or . . . . . . For once he was glad to see the Graber children coming down the road.

As soon as he was on the buggy, he began telling them what he had seen. Freeman turned his head and said, "It was probably a bear," then he laughed and laughed.

Abner laughed too, but the girls only smiled, and Elsie said, "It probably isn't anything that would hurt you."

But Sammie was sure he had seen something. And it had moved so it must be alive.

Chapter 24

Sammie's Fear

That afternoon when Mrs. McPhail dismissed the students, Sammie didn't want to go home. All the rest of the pupils got their hats and bonnets and lunchboxes and, talking and shouting as they usually did, they left the yard. Finally, everyone else was gone and the Graber children were still sitting on the buggy waiting for Sammie. He had not yet come out of the coat room. He was fiddling with his lunchbox and toying with his hat.

Mrs. McPhail came to see what was keeping him. Squatting down in front of him and studying his face, she asked. "What is wrong, Sammie?"

He longed to tell her that he was scared to go home and how he wished there was another way to get there besides walking up that gravel road past the old farm, but Sammie couldn't express himself very well in English, and Mrs. McPhail spoke no German. When he tried to talk, a lump came to his throat, and no words came out of his mouth.

"Come, they are waiting for you," she said as she gently took him by the hand and led him outside to the waiting buggy. She chatted pleasantly as she helped him on the front seat with Freeman and Abner.

Surprisingly, Freeman moved over and made room. After all, he couldn't resist with the teacher right there, but he ignored Sammie and, paying strict attention to his driving, grabbed the whip and started the horse. When they reached the road, he turned north. One-half mile and he turned left. He again whipped the horse across the flank. It laid back its ears like usual, but kept up a good fast trot the whole three miles to Walnut Corners. There they turned north again. One-fourth mile and it was time for Sammie to get down and walk home.

The buggy stopped, but Sammie didn't move. "Get off!" Freeman ordered. He waited a bit, and then gave Sammie a push. "Get off!" he insisted again.

But Sammie still didn't move. He knew he had seen something that morning. How could he walk past that place now? His lower lip quivered. He fought to keep the tears from coming.

"Get off, I said!" Freeman yelled. He took the leather driving lines and began whipping Sammie across the legs.

Now Sammie did move. He was crying as he slowly climbed from the buggy. As he stepped back from the wheel, he again remembered what had scared him that morning, and stopped.

Abner followed him off the buggy and half struck and half pushed him saying, "Go home!"

Now a new feeling welled up inside Sammie, and suddenly he was angry. When Freeman had whipped him, he had felt subdued, but Abner was closer to his age, and he wanted to hurt him. He would chase Abner back onto the buggy where he belonged, he thought! Sammie wound up to bring his lunchbox down on Abner's head, but stopped. Freeman had seen what Sammie was about to do, and was coming down over the buggy wheel. Sammie didn't wait. He turned and ran!

When he looked back, the Grabers were driving away. Now he was alone. The old abandoned farmstead lay between him and home, and he would have to walk past it.

He walked until he was almost to the old farm, and then began running. He kept his eyes straight ahead and

ran as fast as his little bare feet would carry him until he was well past the bridge. By this time, his breath was coming in gasps, and he had to stop to rest. He looked back, but nothing was following him.

He wiped his tears, walked past the woods and on up the gravel road, and soon was home. How he wished he could stay there. On the little farm he felt safe and secure. Dad and Mom were there, and Queen and Sport, and all the other familiar things, too. He didn't mind the work at all. He'd carry wood, or feed calves, or whatever Dad and Mom asked, he'd do without complaint. He'd do those things all day if only they would let him stay home from school.

A truck was at the farm to pick up tomatoes. It was a cool fall day and patches of clouds moved across the sky.

"If it clears off, we could have frost tonight," Dad said.

The pickers were working long and hard to get all the ripe tomatoes harvested before nightfall, because after the frost hit, they would be no good.

Mom was hurrying to get things in from the garden, too. She picked the last of the green string beans, put the stalks of celery into the root cellar, and loaded the peppers into a bushel basket and set them in the wash house.

"The potatoes and the cabbage we'll leave out yet," she told the children. "Those things don't mind a little frost. Just so we harvest them before the ground freezes."

She sent the children to the field to pick the green and partly ripe tomatoes the pickers had left on the vines. "Try to pick all the ones that have some red on them," Mom said. "Those will finish ripening inside the house."

Sammie and Lydia set a basket on the little red wagon and went to the field. So many tomatoes had been left behind that, with Sammie pulling the wagon and Lydia picking, they had no trouble quickly filling the basket. The Mexicans were working swiftly and chattering away in Spanish. The children stopped and listened for a while, and then went on. The sun dropped lower in the sky, and it became colder. Sammie and Lydia's bare feet were cold, so Sammie, using a stick, stirred up some earth and they both buried their feet in the still-warm soil for a few minutes.

When the basket was full, Sammie and Lydia pulled the little wagon to the wash house. Mom put the green tomatoes on the window sill, where they would ripen in the sun, and give them juicy red tomatoes even after everything on the outside had frozen. While this wasn't very important to Dad, the rest of the family loved tomatoes!

"Yep, I think it is going to freeze tonight," Dad said when he came in for supper. The wind had died down and it was getting colder. "Too bad we can't harvest any more of those tomatoes. There are quite a few green ones left on the vines."

Sure enough, the next morning frost lay cold and glittering all over the little farm. White crystals were on the grass and the roofs and the garden plants and the cornfields. Everything would change now. All the flowers along the edge of Mom's garden would turn drab and black, and the corn would turn brown and dry out.

It was too cold to go barefoot, so Sammie put on socks and his old shoes to go to the barn. The shoes pinched his feet and there were holes in the side, but it was better than having cold feet.

"That's the end of the tomato harvest," Dad said when Mom and Sammie came into the barn.

"Yes," Mom agreed. "It was a pretty good crop."

"Yes, it was," Dad said. "If only they had started picking earlier, we could easily have shipped twice as many tomatoes as we did."

"Oh well," Mom answered, "We couldn't help it. At least we will get something out of it."

Mom milked her cows, and Sammie did his chores. When Mom went to the house, Sammie went along because it was time to get ready for school. He thought and thought as he changed his clothes, and by the time he sat down at the table for breakfast, he had a bad feeling in his stomach.

"Eat your cereal, Sammie," Mom urged. Sammie looked at it but could not eat. Mom looked him over. She lay the back of her hand on his forehead.

"What is wrong, Sammie?" she asked.

One minute he wanted to tell Mom what the problem was, and the next he didn't. Suppose she would think his fears were silly, too, like the Graber boys did. Suppose she'd laugh and tell him to go on to school. Finally he said, "My stomach doesn't feel good, I don't w-w-want to go to school."

She studied his face. Again she laid the back of her hand on his forehead.

"You don't have a fever," she said. She went to the medicine cabinet and got a bottle of pink medicine.

"This should settle your stomach," she said, giving him a large spoonful. But medicine didn't help. Sammie still didn't want to go to school.

When Dad came in from the barn, he checked Sammie over to see what the trouble could be. As he began asking questions, Sammie started to cry. Dad kept looking at him. Sammie didn't cry like a boy who was sick. He didn't cry like a boy who had pain. He cried like a boy who was in trouble.

And Sammie was in trouble! He didn't know what Dad would do if he told his problem. He supposed that Dad might scold him and send him on to school, but he didn't want to walk past that abandoned farmstead. He didn't want to ride with the Graber children, either. He just couldn't and he just wouldn't.

"Now, now, Sammie don't cry," Dad said. "Tell me what is bothering you. Did the teacher have to punish you or something?"

Sammie shook his head.

"Are you crying about your old shoes?" Dad asked. Again Sammie shook his head.

"Do you have trouble getting along with your schoolmates?" Dad questioned. Sammie started to shake his head, then hesitated.

Dad kept on questioning and Sammie began talking. The more he said, the easier it was. Finally, Dad had heard the whole story.

"Did you strike back when Freeman whipped you with the lines?" Dad asked.

"No," Sammie answered. He hoped Dad would never find out how much he had wanted to hit Abner, though.

"Well, I hope you didn't. You must never hit others, not even if they strike you first," Dad said.

Dad looked at the clock, looked again at Sammie, and then turned to Mom and said, "He's too late to catch his ride. Maybe he had better stay home. What do you think?"

"Probably so," Mom answered.

Sammie could hardly believe how things were turning out. He felt like jumping and whooping with all his might. But he stayed quiet for fear that Dad and Mom might still change their minds.

Now Sammie felt much better. The color came back into his cheeks. The bad feeling in his stomach was gone. He sat down at the table with the rest of the family and ate a good hearty breakfast.

Chapter 25

Solving the Problem

After breakfast, Dad hitched Queen to the buggy and went driving down the gravel road to Orin Grabers.

Sammie and Lydia helped Mom with the breakfast dishes, and then put on their wraps and went out to play.

The sun was out and it was getting warmer. Where the sun hit, the frost was gone. The frost itself had been sparkling and beautiful, but now in its place were drab, black-looking plants.

Only yesterday the zinnias and petunias and marigolds and the rooster's comb and the snow-on-the-mountain were fresh and pretty, but now they all hung their heads and looked sad.

Just before noon Dad came driving home again. The children followed him as he put Queen in the stable and gave her some oats. Then they followed him to the mailbox and on into the house.

Mom had dinner on the table and everything smelled good. She had made mashed potatoes and gravy and fried chicken and sweet corn cooked in a thick sauce. Sammie and Lydia had brought apple sauce and peaches from the root cellar. Mom had also made graham cracker pudding and had sliced a heaping plate-full of ripe tomatoes. Of course there was good homemade bread and blackberry jelly. It was almost like company dinner.

Sammie spooned out a little of everything and ate it all. Dad and Mom had to help the other children because they were smaller. But Sammie was six years old, and he could help himself. He could spread his own jelly and everything.

Sometimes the little children couldn't eat everything on their plates. When that happened, Dad told them, "Push back your plate if you are full." But Mom had said that it wasn't good manners to leave food, and since Sammie was now six years old, he was old enough to practice good manners. When they were finished eating, his plate was as clean as Dad's.

"I went on over to the canning factory and picked up the tomato check," Dad said, pushing back his chair, "I think I will take it right to the bank this afternoon. Do you need anything in town?"

"The children need shoes," Mom answered.

"Well," Dad said, looking around the table, "Why don't you get ready and we'll all go."

The children jumped up and down with joy. They were all going to town! Sammie and Lydia chipped right in and helped with the dishes without having to be told, and in no time at all the kitchen was clean. They changed into clean clothes, and Mom washed their faces so that, when Queen and the buggy appeared in front of the house, everyone was ready to go.

They drove down the highway past all the farms and fields and woodlots. Soon they passed the James' place with its large letters on the barn roof. From there they could see the tops of the tall grain elevators at the two feed mills. Sammie and Lydia tried to be the first to see the houses of town. Sammie was sure he had seen them first, but Lydia was too. They argued about it until Mom told them to quit the nonsense.

Dad guided Queen up the side street on the east side of town, and turned left into a large parking lot. Along one side was a long hitching rail to which he tied Queen, this time with the neck rope!

The hitching rail was behind a row of store buildings. The bank, the hardware store, and the general store were in one row, and together took up one whole city block. On the very end of the row was the lumber yard, which took up a whole block by itself. All those places had their tall red brick fronts on Main Street and a concrete sidewalk that ran past their doors.

Mom and the children waited outside while Dad went into the bank. When he came out, they all walked to the general store. Dad said it was a general store because they sold everything from food to clothing to toys. There were so many things in that store that Sammie couldn't see everything. Some shelves reached even higher than Dad's head.

Their first stop was in the shoe department. The salesman showed Sammie where to sit, measured his foot, and then took a long stick with something that worked like fingers on the end and used it to reach high up on a shelf to bring down a box of shoes. He slipped one shoe over Sammie's foot and felt around the toes.

"We want them large enough to allow for growing," Dad said.

The man put those shoes back in the box and got down another pair. These shoes felt better. They didn't pinch his feet anywhere. Dad felt around the toes and nodded his head, then looked at the price tag on the box. The shoes cost $2.19, which was a lot of money, but they were good quality and would last.

"Now, we need some overshoes to go over them," Dad said.

The man took out one of the shoes and fitted it with a black rubber boot with four buckles down the front.

Next Lydia and Dannie were fitted with shoes and overshoes. Theirs weren't as expensive as Sammie's because they were smaller, but altogether it cost a lot of money to get both new shoes and new overshoes for three children. It was a good thing that Dad had gotten the tomato check.

Now Mom went to the grocery section and picked out the things she needed. When she had placed everything on the counter, Dad asked, "Is there anything else we want?" Mom shook her head "no", but Dad walked back to the freezer anyway and took out a square cardboard box of ice cream.

"Can we afford it?" Mom asked when Dad returned to the counter. "Oh, for once, I guess," Dad answered, as he paid for everything.

It was time to go back to the buggy, and each of the children carried something. Mom carried Baby David, and Dad had almost everything else in his arms. Sammie made sure that what he was carrying was his new shoes and boots!

Dad opened the back curtain of the buggy and put the bags of groceries and their other things inside. Then they all got on the buggy and drove toward home.

Sammie sat thinking. Why did he have to go to school? What would happen the next morning? Dad had not told him anything when he came home from the Grabers. Sammie liked the way things were right now. The family was together. Queen was clop-clopping down the road as she always did. There was going to be store-bought ice cream for supper. Sammie was happy, and he wished that time would not move on.

After chores the next morning, Mom told Sammie to change into his school clothes. He looked at her, and the bad feeling started again in his stomach.

"Go on," Mom said, "Dad will walk with you to the corner."

Now that made a difference! He felt much better already and got dressed in a hurry.

The sun was still low in the eastern sky when Dad and Sammie walked down the gravel road. This morning the woods didn't seem nearly as dark, and the abandoned farmstead didn't look nearly as scary. Dad was walking next to him and nothing could hurt him.

Dad turned in at the driveway, and they walked across the yard through the tall grass. Weeds grew right up to the porch, and the front door hung on one hinge.

"I think this is what you saw," Dad said, pointing to a piece of tar paper stuck to a branch of a small tree just inside the hedge.

Sammie smiled sheepishly.

"It probably blew down from the roof," Dad continued, pointing up to the housetop, and went on. "It was windy that morning, and this probably went up and down like this." He pushed the branch up and down with his hand.

It all made sense. If he had looked a bit longer, no doubt he would have seen what it was, but he had been scared and hadn't bothered to inspect that black thing.

"Anyway," Dad went on, "There is nothing on this place that will hurt you. You can walk past here by yourself, but you can't let your imagination play tricks on you."

They went back out on the road and walked to the corner. Soon the Graber children came driving along and stopped.

"Good morning!" Dad greeted them.

The girls smiled and said a cheery "good morning". Freeman and Abner didn't say anything, but they lifted the blanket and made room for Sammie on the front seat.

For once Freeman started the horse without the whip, and they went down the road toward school.

After that Sammie always rode in front with the boys, and Abner became more friendly as time went on. Freeman did no more mean things; he simply ignored Sammie.

But every time Sammie walked past the old abandoned farmstead, he had to fight the feeling of fear. His imagination wanted to "play tricks on him," as Dad had explained it, but he forced himself to walk on and tried to remember that Dad said nothing was there that could hurt him.

Chapter 26

Dad Goes Away

At night Sammie heard Dad and Mom talking. The tomato check had helped them get shoes and other necessities, and Dad had caught up with some of the bills and bought things he needed on the farm. But only half the tomato crop had been sold. The rest had rotted in the field.

"I'm not interested in another year like this," Dad said. "It looks plain as day to me that it is time to do something else."

But Mom didn't know. She liked the farm, and she was used to the flat prairies of Indiana.

"Maybe you're homesick," she said. "I know we had a lot of bad luck this year, but things seem to always work out somehow. Maybe a vacation back to your homefolk's would help."

One day soon after, Dad went away. When Sammie came home from school, Dad was gone. Mom told him that Dad had gone on the train back where he had lived as a boy. He would eat and sleep at Grandfather's house and, in a few days, he'd be home again.

But the little farm was lonely without Dad. There was a strange and empty feeling when they sat down to eat. Twice a day, Allen Graber came across the fields to do chores. He was a good helper and made sure everything was cared for, but it wasn't like having Dad at home.

On Saturday, Uncle Andy came. He talked with Mom for a long time. He was sad because he had heard that Dad had gone to Ohio to look for a new home.

A new home! Sammie was all ears now! Would they leave the little farm? He stayed close by to hear what they were saying, but Mom said, "Go outside and play, Sammie."

He knew what that meant. Whatever they were talking about wasn't meant for his ears. He desperately wanted to hear more, but he had to mind Mom. He went outside with Lydia and Dannie. They began playing with the wagon, but very soon, all three were sitting on the wagon talking. They looked around the farm. Would they soon be leaving it all? Dannie said he didn't want to live in another house. Lydia hoped there was a swing to play with if they moved. Sammie thought and thought.

Moving far away sounded exciting! There would be new things to do and it would probably be in the hills which Dad had often talked about. But what would happen to all the things on the little farm? Sammie didn't want to leave all that.

When Uncle Andy left, they went back into the house. Mom was in the kitchen making dinner and singing:

Trau auf Gott in allen sachen,	*Trust in God in all things That make you so sad*
Die dich jetz so trauerich machen;	*Trust in God in every instance*
Trau auf Gott in allen dingen,	*That presses on your heart.*
Die dir zu den Herzen dringen.	

"Mom, are we going to move?" Lydia asked.

"I don't know," Mom answered.

"Well, why did Uncle Andy say something about it then?" Sammie asked.

"Oh well, other people always seem to know more about us than we do. We will all find out soon enough, so be still about it," she told them.

So they were still. At least around Mom. But they kept wondering and wishing all the more that Dad would come home.

The next day was Sunday. There was no church, and the day seemed very long. In the forenoon, Mom told the children stories, and they took turns sitting on Dad's rocking chair. When Dad was home they couldn't do that.

In the afternoon, Sammie and Lydia and Dannie went out to play. It was a beautiful, clear fall day. The leaves were almost all off the trees, and the corn fields were brown and dry. Dad hadn't put any in shocks like he had in past years, and the whole field stood rustling in the autumn breeze.

They played a game which Sammie had learned in school. Sammie lay down on the grass under the oak tree. Lydia and Danny covered him all over with leaves so that he couldn't see, and marched around him singing, "Pop Goes the Weasel." When they came to the word "pop", one of them would punch Sammie, and Sammie would jump up and try to catch the one who had punched him. If he caught the right one, that person had to go under the leaves. If not then he had to be "it" again.

Later they went into the house for popcorn and apples. Finally Allen Graber came walking across the field, and it was chore time.

The next day Dad came home. He was there when Sammie came home from school, and, at suppertime, he told them about his trip.

Grandfather and Grandmother were surprised and happy to see him. He slept and ate at their house, and all his brothers and nieces and nephews came to visit. He had had a nice trip, but the best part was this: He had found a place to move to.

"It is just right for what I have in mind," Dad said. "It is a small place, but I think you'll all like it. The people who own it won't sell, but we can rent it. We can sell this farm and square away our debts. There should be some money left over, too. In time we can buy our own place again. This particular little place is located right smack in the middle of the Amish community where I can build up a business shoeing horses. So, what do you think, Mom?"

"Whatever you think is best," Mom said.

"Well, if you agree, I'll sit right down and write them a letter. We should make up our mind before someone else comes along and beats us to it. I think it is for the best. I'd be glad to get rid of some of these debts, and it seems so much can always go wrong on a farm," Dad said.

"We did have some bad luck this last year," Mom agreed, "but we also have more stock than we had before. With the children growing up, I hate to think about leaving the farm. Sammie is almost seven already."

Dad's face clouded a little, "Well, say we take this chance while it is here. When the children get bigger we can go back to farming if we still want to. Maybe we'd be fixed better financially by that time, too,"

So Mom said no more about staying. She asked questions about the new home and helped Dad plan things about the move.

Sammie was thinking. If they left the farm, what would happen to the horses and cows and calves and pigs and chickens? Who would then live on the little farm?

Dad kept talking, "We can have an auction and sell the farm things."

The farm things? Sammie wondered what all was considered farm things. So he asked, "May we keep Sport?"

"Why sure, Sammie. None of us would think of selling Sport. We'll also keep Queen and the buggy and most of the household things," Dad said.

"May we keep the swing?" Lydia asked.

"Yes, we can put it up somewhere at our new home," Dad answered.

So the planning went on.

One evening when Sammie came home from school, Mom told him to be very quiet. Dad's brother John and his Uncle Jonas had come for the auction. They had traveled during the night and now they were resting.

"Don't wake them," Mom said.

Sammie tip-toed through the house, changed into his chore clothes, and went outdoors. Outside, everything looked strange. Because the auction was tomorrow, the shed was empty. In the hay field, machinery was lined up, ready to be sold. Dad was very busy fixing things and setting them out. Orin Graber, Uncle Andy and Eli Mullet had helped him all day. Now they had gone home, but Dad was still busy.

That night the children got to know their Uncle John and Great Uncle Jonas. They both asked the children the usual questions. Sammie could answer everything they asked because he was older and had more experience. Lydia answered what her name was and her age, but Danny just said his name and held up four fingers to show his age.

Great Uncle Jonas was a very old man. The top of his head was completely bald. He had so few hairs on his head that his hat didn't cover any of them when he wore it, but even so, he combed the silky white locks straight down every time he washed up for a meal.

Great Uncle Jonas was a very kind old man, and Sammie loved to listen to him talk. He told Sammie and Lydia stories while Uncle John bounced Dannie up and down, playing *Reidy, reidy, Geily* (Ride, ride, horsey).

Then Great Uncle Jonas took out some pink Doddy candy and gave the children each a piece. It had a sweet mint flavor.

Sammie remembered his manners and said "thank you" before even tasting the candy. Lydia also said, "Thank you," and Danny said it after Dad helped him. Baby David couldn't talk so Mom said "Thank you" for him. She cut his candy in pieces so it wouldn't get stuck in his throat.

While the children were eating their candy, Uncle John played another game with them, in which he checked each of the children to see if they had stolen sheep. This is how he did it. He tickled their knee, and if they squirmed, he said they had stolen sheep. No matter how hard Sammie tried, he couldn't keep from squirming.

Finally he reached up and tickled Uncle John's knee. But no amount of tickling made him squirm.

"That is because I didn't steal any sheep," Uncle John said, laughing.

Then Mom said it was bedtime for the children. The trick playing and story telling had to come to an end.

Sammie settled in his bed upstairs and listened. The hum-drum of the visiting floated up to him from downstairs. He tried to catch the words, but they were too far away. He thought about Great Uncle Jonas. Maybe some day he would be a very old man like Jonas. He'd want to be nice and kind, too, and remember to tell stories to little children like Jonas did.

Then he thought about moving. If they moved to Ohio, they would get to see Jonas more often. That was one good thing. The voices downstairs drifted away and Sammie was fast asleep.

the hall to the room Ivey shared with Vicki. They moved so quietly that not even the floorboards creaked. The house was quiet. The voice was still. Jason was the only one still awake.

Chapter 27

Leaving the Little Farm

The next morning Sammie didn't have to go to school. By mid-morning there were people all around — both neighbors who were there to help and people who had come for the auction. Everywhere he went, Sammie encountered strange people, and it made him uncomfortable. Cy Ziegler was the auctioneer. He had a big voice, and Sammie felt small when Cy talked to him, but Dad liked Cy, so Sammie did, too.

When the time came to start the auction, Cy Ziegler climbed on the wagon and began selling Dad's things. He sold lots of small items off the wagon, then he sold the wagon and the machinery sitting in the hay field. He sold the hay and the oats and the barley in the granary and the corn still standing in the field. By that time it was afternoon, and the livestock was next. He sold the pigs and the cows and the calves and the chickens and Mollie and Dollie and Tim. Finally, he even sold the farm.

Then came the hardest part. People began leaving with Dad's things and Dad's animals. They loaded cows and calves and pigs on trucks, and Sammie saw a man lead Rose, the brindle cow, away.

Uncle Andy bought Tim, and Sammie was glad. He would work with Tim like Dad had. Uncle Andy was a good horseman, and Tim would have a good home. But Orin Graber bought Mollie and Dollie. Sammie watched him lead them away across the highway and down the gravel road until they were out of sight, and felt sorry for them.

Finally all the people were gone except Cy Ziegler. Soon he left too, and the family was alone. Even Uncle John and Great Uncle Jonas had left on a train to go back to their home in Ohio. The farm felt still and empty. All the cows and calves were gone. The chicken houses were empty and there were no pigs left in the pen. Only Queen still stood in the barn munching her hay.

Dad gave Queen her measure of grain, and the chores were done. There was nothing else to do, so Dad and Sammie went to the house. Sport, who was lying in front of the steps, wagged his tail. He looked at Sammie with his sad brown eyes and whimpered. A heavy feeling came over Sammie, and even Dad looked a little gloomy.

After supper, Dad sat in his rocking chair holding Dannie. Sammie brought his little bench and sat close by.

"Dad," he began.

"What do you want, Sammie?" Dad asked.

"Dad, don't you wish someone else would have bought Mollie and Dollie?" Sammie asked.

Dad thought a little, then he said, "Sammie, it was a public auction. Everybody had the right to buy. Orin paid for Mollie and Dollie, and they belong to him now."

"But the Grabers are so rough with horses," Sammie said.

"Well, we shouldn't talk too much about other peoples' faults, because we have our own, too," Dad explained.

"I still wish someone else had bought Mollie and Dollie," Sammie insisted.

"Don't worry, Sammie," Dad said, "They'll probably sell them again, anyway. The Grabers like wild horses, and Mollie and Dollie are tame. That is probably why Orin bought them to start with. They have plenty of horses."

That made Sammie feel a bit better.

Then Dad told them all about the place they were moving to. It wasn't a farm, but there was plenty of room for the children to play.

"I will have to build a bridge so we can get to the barn with dry feet. A creek runs between the house and barn," Dad said. "There's also a building there which I can use for a shop. That way I can start shoeing horses immediately."

Dad told them that they would be able to visit Grandfather and Grandmother in the buggy, and that there were many uncles and aunts and cousins living nearby. There were nice neighbors, and Sammie's school wasn't far. But now, Dad said, it was bed time, and the talking and planning had to stop.

As Sammie settled into his bed, a thousand thoughts raced through his mind. So much had happened so fast, however, that he could not think about everything at once, and he was very tired. Mom was singing softly as she rocked Little David, and it wasn't long before Sammie fell asleep listening to Mom's clear voice singing:

> *Precious memories, how they linger,*
> *How they ever flood my soul!*
> *In the stillness of the midnight*
> *Precious, sacred scenes unfold.*

Two trucks arrived very early in the morning on moving day. Neighbors came to help, and everything was packed quickly. The beds were taken apart and the pieces were loaded onto one truck. The wheels were taken off the buggy so that it would not take up so much room, and it was hoisted onto the other truck. Queen was led onto the truck bed, and stood whinnying, impatient to get going.

Uncle Andys were there, and Aunt Lena helped Mom get things together. The morning was frosty, and everybody worked in the cold because the stoves were already packed on the trucks. As the sun climbed higher, however, the day became warmer.

"We must be getting our Indian summer," Uncle Andy said.

When Sammie had a chance, he asked Dad what an Indian summer was.

"Oh," Dad explained, "almost every year we get some nice sunny days after the hard frosts and cool weather. People call those days Indian summer."

"Indian Summer." Sammie liked to say it. Today he had learned another new word.

The trucks were almost loaded when, suddenly, Lydia tugged at Dad's pantleg.

"What do you want, Lydia?" Dad asked.

"Dad, the swing is still on the tree," she said.

"Oh, yes, the swing." Dad had forgotten. The ladder was already on the truck, but he took it off, propped it against the oak tree, and in a minute the swing was down and safely on board.

Now everything was ready to go. Sport was in a cage at the back end of one truck so that he could see out. He didn't like it, but that could not be helped. Before evening, he would again be able to run around at their new home.

Mom and Aunt Lena had made sandwiches and sliced carrots and celery which they packed, along with other eats, into a basket.

"We can stop somewhere along the way for a picnic," Mom said. "By noon the weather will be nice and warm. Maybe we can even stop and buy some ice cream to go with this food." Then she looked at Sammie and continued, "We will find some way to celebrate. We have a birthday in the family today."

Sammie looked back at Mom. He had forgotten! Today was his birthday! He was seven years old. Store-bought ice cream for lunch! He couldn't wait!

Sammie and Lydia returned to the house for one last look. The rooms were empty and hollow, and it didn't seem like home anymore. They went back outside where Dad and the truck drivers were tying the loads down with rope.

Neighbors and friends were saying their goodbyes.

"We will miss you," Uncle Andy said as he shook all of their hands, even Little David's.

"Be sure to write," Aunt Lena said, wiping a tear with her apron.

Dad helped Mom and Lydia and Little David into the passenger side of the one truck.

"You'll follow us," he told the driver.

He and Sammie and Dannie got in next to the driver of the other truck. Everybody called their last goodbyes, and the driver started the engine. As Sammie sat there listening to the idling motor, he thought. How would it be to live somewhere else? How would it seem to sleep in another house? Surely he would miss the little farm. But Mom had remembered his birthday even if it was moving day, and that gave him a warm feeling. Mom would go on being Mom, and Dad would go on being Dad, regardless where they lived. Lydia, Dannie, and Little David would be there to play with, and Sport would wag his tail like before.

He remembered Queen on the back of the truck. She would again look at him with her gentle eyes and sniff for oats with her pink nose. They would hitch her to the buggy and go visit Great Uncle Jonas or the grandparents or Uncle Johns. The whole family would like that.

Dad had told him that school was only a mile away. There was no abandoned farmstead to walk past, and he wouldn't have to ride with anyone. Suddenly he was eager to see the new home.

"How long will it take to get there?" Sammie asked.

"Are you in a hurry, Sammie?" Dad asked, smiling. "By evening we should be together in our new house."

Sammie smiled back. He knew he wanted to be where Dad and Mom were. "No other place would seem like home, not even the little farm," Sammie thought.

The trucks began moving. They stopped at the road to let some traffic pass. Then they pulled out and headed east. Sammie stretched to get one more look at the farm. He wondered if he would ever see it again.

Appendix

Recipes

Halfmoon Pies

2 quarts schnitz (dried apples)
3 cups water
3 cups sugar
¾ tsp. cinnamon

Wash the schnitz and add 3 cups of water. Cover and cook
until soft and the water is taken up. Add the sugar and the
cinnamon and cook ten more minutes. Stir until it is
smooth. If you want it really smooth, put it through a ricer.
Set it aside to cool.

Pie Dough

3 cups pastry flour
1 tsp. salt
1 cup lard
¾ cup hot water (boiling)

Combine flour and salt and mix in lard. Mix well. Add hot
water a little at a time and work it in. Handle the dough as
little as possible after the water is added.

Break off a piece of dough the size of a walnut. Roll it
out (as thin as you prefer). Mark half of the dough and on
one side place a heaping tablespoon of cooked schnitz. Fold
it over, shaping it like a half moon. Crimp the edges and
cut off the excess dough. Bake in oven at 400 degrees.

Dandelion Gravy

1 cup of chopped dandelion greens
3 hard boiled eggs
3 slices fried bacon

Chop these all into small pieces and set aside to be added after the gravy is made. Save the bacon grease to be used in making the gravy.

2 Tbs. flour
¾ cup water
¾ cup milk
1 tsp. salt
2 Tbs. vinegar

Put the bacon grease and a little butter into a large skillet. Add the flour and heat until it is well browned. Then slowly pour in the water, while stirring with a spatula to keep smooth. When that reaches a bubbling boil, add the milk, again stirring to keep it smooth. If the gravy is too thick, add a little water. If it is too thin, add a sauce of flour and water. When it returns to a bubbling boil, it is done.

Take from the heat and add the eggs, the bacon, the salt, the vinegar, and the dandelion greens.

Sausage Seasoning

10 lbs. ground pork
5 rounded Tbsp. salt
1 tsp. sage
4 tsp. pepper (white or black)
2 tsp. dry mustard powder

Mix well into the meat and form into patties or stuff in casings.

Rivvel Soup

1 quart milk
1 teaspoon salt
1 egg yolk
3 tablespoons flour

Bring milk to a boil without scorching. Make rivvels by combining egg yolk and flour and chopping until the pieces are 1/4 inch or less. Stir rivvels into the boiling milk a little at a time. Simmer for 3 minutes and remove from heat. For thicker soup, make more rivvels.

Tomato Gravy

1 pint water
1 pint tomato juice
1 tsp. salt.

Sauce:
1 cup milk
¼ cup flour

Combine water, tomato juice and salt. Bring to a boil. Slowly add the milk/flour sauce, stirring continuously.. Simmer for a few minutes and serve. More or less sauce may be used to thin or thicken the gravy. Serve over fried cornmeal mush.

About the Author

Noah Hershberger grew up in a large Amish community in Ohio. He received his formal education in a one room parochial school and has become a teacher in that system.

Mr. Hershberger presently lives with his family in Southwestern Wisconsin on a "little farm" similar to the one described in this book. He is kept busy teaching, writing and farming.